2030 THE ANUNNAKI RETURN

Carlos T Dawring

Copyright © 2024 Carlos T Dawring

All rights reserved

The characters and events portrayed in this book are fictitious. Any similarity to real persons, living or dead, is coincidental and not intended by the author.

No part of this book may be reproduced, or stored in a retrieval system, or transmitted in any form or by any means, electronic, mechanical, photocopying, recording, or otherwise, without express written permission of the publisher.

ISBN-13: 9798344199412
ISBN-10: 1477123456

Cover design by: Art Painter
Library of Congress Control Number: 2018675309
Printed in the United States of America

CONTENTS

Title Page
Copyright
Chapter 1: A New Discovery — 2
Chapter 2: Ancient Warnings — 14
Chapter 3: The Approach — 27
Chapter 4: The Arrival — 39
Chapter 5: The Negotiations — 52
Chapter 6: Secrets of the Moon — 66
Chapter 7: Mars Unveiled — 78
Chapter 8: Cultural Exchange — 92
Chapter 9: The Gold Rush — 100
Chapter 10: Enki's Vision — 107
Chapter 11: Challenges and Triumphs — 115
Chapter 12: The Mars Colony — 123
Chapter 13: Inanna's Influence — 130
Chapter 14: Uncovering the Past — 139
Chapter 15: Unity and Progress — 147
Chapter 16: The Final Gold Shipment — 155
Chapter 17: A New Dawn — 162
Chapter 18: Legacy of the Anunnaki — 170

CARLOST.DAWRING

2030 - Anunnaki Return

CHAPTER 1: A NEW DISCOVERY

In the summer of 2025, the world changed forever. The night sky over the University of Cambridge Observatory was clear and dark, offering a perfect canvas for the stars to display their brilliance. Dr. Emily Hayes, a renowned astronomer at the observatory, had just settled into her nightly routine. This routine had become a ritual of sorts, a quiet, meditative practice where she could escape the hustle and bustle of daily life. She meticulously scanned the star-studded canvas of the sky, her fingers deftly adjusting the telescope's focus, each subtle movement honed by years of experience. The familiar hum of the observatory's equipment and the gentle whir of the telescope's motors provided a comforting backdrop as she worked.

Her routine had always been a serene escape, a chance to marvel at the cosmic ballet playing out above. Dr. Hayes found solace in the predictability of the stars, each night a reminder of the vastness and constancy of the universe. On this particular night, however, her serenity was shattered. As she peered through the eyepiece, a new celestial body caught her attention. At first, it was faint, almost imperceptible, a mere speck against the inky backdrop. She initially dismissed it as a flicker of light, perhaps a distant satellite or a reflection off some space debris. Yet, something about its movement compelled her to take a closer look.

It moved in a way that defied the predictable paths of known planets and stars. It did not follow the smooth, arched trajectories that she had come to expect from celestial objects. Instead, it darted across the field of view with an urgency that sent a chill down her spine. Her heart pounded as she recalibrated the telescope, ensuring her equipment was not at fault. She adjusted the lens, checked the coordinates, and even recalculated the object's position manually, her mind racing with possibilities.

The object, now clearer, loomed larger and more menacing with each passing moment. It was not a comet or an asteroid, but something far more significant. The rogue planet, with its ominous presence, seemed to hurtle towards the inner solar system at an alarming speed. The size and speed of the celestial body were unlike anything she had ever encountered in her career. Her mind raced with the implications, the potential gravitational effects, and the possible collisions with other celestial bodies.

Dr. Hayes felt a chill run down her spine. She knew she had discovered something monumental, something that would alter the course of human history. Her serene night of stargazing had turned into a night of revelation and fear. The discovery of Nibiru, as she would later name it, marked the beginning of a new chapter for humanity. She quickly gathered her data, her hands trembling with a mix of excitement and dread. This was no ordinary night at the observatory; this was the night the world would change forever.

With a sense of urgency, she began to document her findings, her mind already leaping ahead to the next steps. She would need to alert her colleagues, publish her observations, and prepare for the inevitable media frenzy. But for now, she took a moment to gaze once more at the rogue planet, feeling the weight of the discovery settle upon her shoulders. In that instant, she understood that Nibiru was not just a new celestial body; it was a harbinger of unprecedented change, a cosmic message that would soon echo across the globe.

The following morning, Dr. Hayes's discovery was the talk of the scientific community. Her night of frantic calculations and hurried messages had paid off. As the sun rose, painting the sky in hues of pink and gold, the astronomical world was already abuzz with the news. Dr. Hayes had contacted her colleagues, sharing her detailed observations and data with the precision and clarity for which she was known. Emails, phone calls, and secure transmissions flew across the globe, reaching observatories, universities, and research institutions. The response was immediate and electrifying.

Soon, astronomers around the globe were verifying her findings. Telescopes from Chile to Hawaii, from Japan to South Africa, were trained on the coordinates she had provided. The evidence was irrefutable: Nibiru was real, and it was on a collision course with the inner planets. The implications were staggering. This rogue planet, moving with terrifying speed, threatened to disrupt the delicate balance of our solar system. The scientific implications alone were profound, promising to rewrite textbooks and challenge our understanding of celestial mechanics. But the potential consequences for Earth and humanity were even more dire.

News of the discovery spread like wildfire. Within hours, it had transcended the confines of academia and reached the public. Social media platforms were abuzz with speculation and fear. Hashtags like #Nibiru, #RoguePlanet, and #EndOfTheWorld trended globally. Amateur astronomers and space enthusiasts shared their own observations, while conspiracy theorists spun elaborate narratives. Panic and fascination mingled in equal measure.

Major news outlets interrupted their regular programming to cover the unfolding story. Anchors, normally composed, delivered updates with a mixture of awe and apprehension. Expert panels were hastily assembled, featuring scientists, historians, and even psychologists to help explain and contextualize the discovery. Nibiru dominated headlines, its impending arrival casting a long shadow over the world's collective consciousness. From the smallest villages to the largest cities, people everywhere were talking about the rogue planet.

Governments around the world convened emergency meetings. The potential threat posed by Nibiru required a coordinated global response. Presidents, prime ministers, and chancellors conferred with their top advisors and scientific experts. Secure communications buzzed between nations, as alliances old and new were tested by the unprecedented crisis. Scientists, politicians, and military leaders scrambled to understand the full scope of the situation and to formulate strategies to mitigate any potential impacts.

The urgency of the moment was palpable. Satellite images of Nibiru, grainy yet unmistakable, were analyzed in war rooms and situation centers. Models and simulations were run continuously, projecting possible trajectories and collision scenarios. Would Nibiru merely pass by, causing minor disruptions with its gravitational pull? Or would it collide with a planet, triggering a catastrophic chain of events?

In this high-stakes environment, the need for clear communication and accurate information was paramount. Misinformation and rumors could easily exacerbate the already volatile situation. Governments issued public statements, urging calm and promising that every effort was being made to safeguard humanity. Emergency protocols were reviewed, and contingency plans were drafted.

The world was on edge, united by a shared sense of uncertainty and fear. Yet, amidst the chaos, there was also a burgeoning sense of solidarity. Scientists from rival nations collaborated openly, sharing data and insights. Ordinary citizens reached out to one another, offering support and comfort. Humanity, faced with a potential existential threat, began to rediscover its capacity for cooperation and compassion.

Dr. Hayes, meanwhile, found herself at the center of this maelstrom. Her discovery had sparked a global reckoning, and she was now a key figure in the efforts to understand and respond to Nibiru. She continued her work tirelessly, driven by a sense of duty and a profound awareness of the stakes. Her nights at the observatory were longer than ever, her mind constantly churning with calculations and hypotheses.

As the days turned into weeks, the initial shock of Nibiru's discovery began to give way to a more measured, determined response. The world had been given a stark reminder of its vulnerability, but also of its resilience. Together, humanity faced the unknown, prepared to meet the challenges ahead with courage and unity.

As the days passed, the media frenzy intensified. Every news outlet, from mainstream networks to independent bloggers, clamored for the latest updates on Nibiru. Speculation about the rogue planet's origins and its potential impact on Earth ran rampant, filling the airwaves and cyberspace with a torrent of theories and opinions. The lack of concrete information, coupled with the natural human tendency to fear the unknown, created a fertile ground for the wildest conjectures to take root.

Conspiracy theories flourished, each more sensational than the last. Some claimed Nibiru was an alien craft, a colossal spaceship from a distant galaxy on a mission of unknown intent. Others suggested it was a harbinger of doom, a cosmic omen signaling the end of days. Still, others proposed that Nibiru was a rogue planet, flung into our solar system by some cosmic cataclysm. Every theory, no matter how outlandish, found its audience. Social media platforms became echo chambers for these ideas, with hashtags and viral posts fueling the fire. People shared videos of dubious origin, and forums buzzed with heated debates. The line between fact and fiction blurred as fear and fascination intertwined.

Amidst the chaos, two individuals emerged as voices of

reason and rationality, cutting through the noise with their measured insights. Graham Hancock, an expert in ancient civilizations, offered a historical context that helped frame the discovery in a broader perspective. He drew on his extensive knowledge of ancient texts and legends, many of which spoke of celestial visitors and cataclysmic events. In televised interviews and public lectures, Hancock referenced Sumerian tablets, Mayan prophecies, and Egyptian hieroglyphs, weaving a narrative that linked Nibiru to humanity's distant past. His insights provided a sense of continuity, suggesting that what seemed unprecedented might, in fact, be part of a larger, ancient story. Hancock's calm demeanor and scholarly approach lent credibility to his theories, offering the public a way to understand the crisis beyond the realm of panic and speculation.

Meanwhile, Jordan Peterson, a renowned psychologist, addressed the psychological impact of the discovery. He understood the primal fear that such an event could evoke, recognizing it as an existential threat that tapped into deep-seated anxieties. In his lectures and media appearances, Peterson offered guidance on how to cope with the anxiety and uncertainty. He spoke about the importance of maintaining a sense of normalcy, encouraging people to focus on their daily routines and responsibilities. He emphasized the need for community and connection, advising individuals to support one another and stay grounded in the face of fear.

Peterson's calming presence and analytical approach helped to soothe the public's frayed nerves. He broke down complex psychological responses into understandable terms, providing practical advice for managing stress and fear. His message was clear: while the future was uncertain, humanity had faced and overcome great challenges before. By remaining calm, rational, and united, we could navigate this new threat with resilience and courage.

The contributions of Hancock and Peterson were instrumental

in shaping the public discourse. Their voices rose above the cacophony of speculation, offering clarity and perspective. As the world grappled with the implications of Nibiru, these two men became beacons of hope and understanding. They reminded us that knowledge and wisdom, even in the face of the unknown, could light the way forward.

As days turned into weeks, the initial wave of panic began to subside. The public, guided by the insights of Hancock and Peterson, started to approach the situation with a more measured response. People sought out reliable information, engaged in thoughtful discussions, and prepared themselves for whatever might come. The media, too, began to shift its focus, providing more balanced and informative coverage. The frenzy was far from over, but a semblance of order was beginning to emerge. In the midst of uncertainty, the world found a fragile but growing sense of calm.

Recognizing the need for a comprehensive understanding of Nibiru and its implications, the academic community rallied together in an unprecedented show of collaboration. Interdisciplinary teams were formed, combining the expertise of astronomers, physicists, historians, and psychologists. The urgency of the situation transcended academic boundaries, creating a fertile ground for innovative thinking and collective problem-solving. Leading this charge were three central figures whose unique perspectives proved invaluable in piecing together the puzzle of Nibiru: Dr. Emily Hayes, Graham Hancock, and Jordan Peterson.

Dr. Hayes continued to lead the astronomical efforts, her observations crucial in tracking Nibiru's trajectory. Her nights at the observatory grew longer and more intense, each session yielding new data that was meticulously analyzed. She and her team developed sophisticated models to predict the planet's path, using advanced computational methods to account for variables that could affect its course. Her findings indicated that the rogue planet's path would bring it perilously close to Earth, but the exact consequences were still uncertain. Would it collide with our planet, or would it merely pass by, its gravitational pull causing widespread disruptions? These questions haunted her, driving her to delve deeper into her research with a determination that inspired her colleagues.

Hancock, meanwhile, delved deeper into ancient texts, searching for clues that might shed light on Nibiru's origins and purpose. He immersed himself in the study of Sumerian tablets, Egyptian hieroglyphs, and Mayan codices, his office resembling an archaeological dig site with its stacks of books and scrolls. He unearthed references to the Anunnaki, a race of advanced beings said to have visited Earth in antiquity. These beings, according to the texts, had interacted with humanity, leaving behind a legacy of knowledge and mystery. Hancock's research suggested that Nibiru's return could herald a new chapter in this ancient saga. He hypothesized that the Anunnaki might be returning to oversee a significant transformation, perhaps linked to the very fabric of human civilization.

Hancock's discoveries were shared in scholarly articles, lectures, and conferences, where he captivated audiences with his ability to connect the dots between ancient history and the present crisis. His work offered a narrative that made the phenomenon of Nibiru not just a scientific anomaly but a continuation of humanity's long and storied past. This perspective provided a sense of continuity and meaning, helping people to frame the current events within a larger, more comprehensible context.

Peterson, on the other hand, focused on preparing society for the psychological challenges ahead. Understanding that fear and uncertainty could lead to widespread panic, he took to the airwaves and the internet to offer guidance. He conducted interviews, wrote articles, and gave public lectures, all aimed at helping people navigate their fears and uncertainties. His message was clear: while the future was uncertain, humanity had faced and overcome great challenges before. By remaining calm and rational, we could face this new threat with resilience and courage.

Peterson emphasized the importance of maintaining social cohesion and mental health during times of crisis. He encouraged people to seek solace in community, to support one another, and to keep a sense of normalcy in their daily lives. His practical advice on coping mechanisms, such as mindfulness and structured routines, resonated with millions who were grappling with the emotional impact of Nibiru's impending arrival. He also worked closely with governmental and non-governmental organizations to develop public health strategies aimed at mitigating the psychological effects of the crisis.

The combined efforts of Dr. Hayes, Hancock, and Peterson created a multifaceted approach to understanding and responding to Nibiru. Dr. Hayes's precise astronomical observations provided the hard data needed to anticipate physical impacts. Hancock's historical and mythological research offered a narrative framework that made sense of the existential threat. Peterson's psychological insights helped manage the collective anxiety, fostering a resilient and prepared populace.

As the interdisciplinary teams continued their work, a clearer picture of Nibiru began to emerge. Collaborative efforts led to breakthroughs in understanding the planet's composition, its potential effects on Earth's climate and tectonics, and its historical significance. The global academic community, galvanized by the leadership of Hayes, Hancock, and Peterson, demonstrated the power of human ingenuity and cooperation in the face of an unprecedented challenge. Together, they worked tirelessly to unlock the secrets of Nibiru, aiming to turn a potential catastrophe into an opportunity for growth and unity.

As summer turned to autumn, the world remained on edge. Nibiru's approach dominated every aspect of life, infiltrating scientific discussions, political debates, and everyday conversations. No topic seemed too trivial or too grand to be overshadowed by the looming celestial visitor. In universities, researchers feverishly worked on models and predictions, while in homes, families discussed contingency plans over dinner. Schools incorporated lessons about space and planetary science into their curricula, and children marveled at the mysteries of the universe, their imaginations sparked by the real-life drama unfolding above.

Governments continued to strategize, preparing for a range of possible scenarios with an urgency that reflected the gravity of the situation. High-level meetings were held in secure locations, where experts from diverse fields presented their findings and proposed solutions. Emergency drills were conducted in cities around the globe, reminiscent of wartime preparations but on a scale that spanned continents. Shelters were reinforced, evacuation routes were mapped out, and communication networks were tested and retested. Resources were stockpiled with a focus on essentials: food, water, medical supplies, and energy reserves. Contingency plans were meticulously detailed, addressing everything from infrastructure damage to economic disruption, and even potential social unrest.

Despite the pervasive tension, there were moments of hope and solidarity that shone through the anxiety. Communities came together, supporting one another in ways that transcended national and cultural boundaries. In neighborhoods, people organized mutual aid groups, ensuring that the elderly and vulnerable had access to necessities. Volunteers set up community centers where information was shared, and where people could find solace in the company of others facing the same fears. Religious and spiritual leaders offered comfort and guidance, reminding their congregations of the resilience and compassion that humanity was capable of.

The shared experience of facing an existential threat fostered a sense of global unity, a powerful reminder of our common humanity. People across the world found themselves united by a common purpose, as borders and political differences became less significant in the face of a planetary crisis. Social media, often a source of division, transformed into a platform for solidarity, with people sharing resources, offering support, and spreading messages of hope. International organizations, from the United Nations to grassroots movements, coordinated efforts to ensure that no region faced the threat alone.

Dr. Hayes, Hancock, and Peterson became symbols of this unity, their collaboration a testament to the power of knowledge and cooperation. Dr. Hayes's relentless dedication to tracking Nibiru provided the world with crucial information, while Hancock's deep dives into ancient texts offered context and a narrative that connected past, present, and future. Peterson's guidance on managing fear and maintaining psychological resilience helped keep the public grounded and focused. Together, they navigated the complex web of scientific discovery, historical interpretation, and psychological resilience, guiding humanity through the uncertainties of this new era.

Their efforts were supported by a vast network of scientists, historians, and mental health professionals, all contributing to a greater understanding of Nibiru and its implications. Televised briefings and online seminars kept the public informed and engaged, demystifying the science and history behind the rogue planet. Educational campaigns were launched to dispel myths and provide clear, accurate information, helping to quell the tide of misinformation that had initially surged.

As Nibiru drew ever closer, the world watched and waited, bracing for whatever the future might hold. The anticipation was palpable, a collective breath held in suspense. Telescopes around the globe were trained on the night sky, capturing images of the approaching planet that were shared in real-time, turning the world's gaze upward. In classrooms and living rooms, people followed the updates with a mix of fear and wonder, knowing that they were living through a moment that would be studied and remembered for generations to come.

The stage was set for an unprecedented encounter, one that would forever alter the course of human history. In this heightened state of awareness and preparedness, humanity stood at the precipice of a new chapter. The lessons learned during this time, the importance of unity, the value of knowledge, and the strength found in resilience, would shape the future in ways both profound and unforeseen. As the clock ticked down to Nibiru's closest approach, the world held its breath, united in hope and resolve, ready to face whatever the cosmos had in store.

CHAPTER 2: ANCIENT WARNINGS

Graham Hancock sat in his cluttered study, surrounded by piles of ancient texts and artifacts, when the call came. The mid-afternoon sunlight filtered through the dusty windows, casting long shadows over his workspace. Manuscripts, scrolls, and fragments of pottery lay strewn across his desk, each piece a testament to his life's work in uncovering the mysteries of ancient civilizations. The ringing phone interrupted his deep concentration on a particularly intricate Sumerian tablet.

The voice on the other end was calm but urgent, requesting his immediate presence in London. It was a high-ranking government official, someone Hancock had only dealt with peripherally in his career. The details were sparse, but the gravity of the situation was clear from the tone. This was not a routine consultation or academic query; this was something far more pressing. "We need you in London, now," the voice said, leaving no room for hesitation.

An hour later, Hancock was on a train, his mind racing through the implications of what he might be called to discuss. The rhythmic clatter of the train wheels did little to soothe his restless thoughts. He replayed the conversation in his head, analyzing every word and inflection. What could be so urgent? His mind darted to the recent news about Nibiru, the rogue planet hurtling towards the inner solar system. Could there be a connection?

Upon arrival in London, Hancock was whisked away by a

government car waiting at the station. The ride was swift and silent, the driver offering no conversation. Hancock noted the heightened security, the way they bypassed regular traffic, moving with a sense of purpose. They arrived at a nondescript building in a secluded part of the city, far from the bustling streets of central London. He was escorted inside, through a maze of corridors and security checkpoints, until they reached a large, dimly lit conference room.

The room was filled with high-ranking officials and scientists, their expressions grave. There were faces he recognized from media briefings and academic conferences, but many were unfamiliar, adding to the air of mystery and tension. The atmosphere was thick with anticipation and concern, a silent acknowledgment of the unprecedented times they were living through. Hancock was ushered to the front, where a large screen displayed a rotating 3D model of Nibiru, along with ancient symbols and text excerpts.

Taking a deep breath, Hancock began to present his findings on the ancient Sumerian texts. He used a laser pointer to highlight key sections of the cuneiform tablets, explaining their significance. The audience listened intently as he spoke of the Anunnaki, a race of advanced beings from Nibiru who, according to the texts, had visited Earth thousands of years ago. He described their arrival, their advanced technology, and their impact on early human civilization.

The Anunnaki had allegedly manipulated human DNA to create a labor force to mine gold, a revelation that cast a new light on the current crisis. Hancock showed images of the texts detailing the genetic experiments, the creation of humans with enhanced abilities for mining. He explained how gold was not just a commodity for the Anunnaki, but a vital resource for their survival, used to stabilize their planet's atmosphere.

As Hancock spoke, he could see the expressions of the officials and scientists shift from skepticism to a mix of awe and concern. The connections he drew between ancient history and the present crisis were compelling, offering a perspective that was both enlightening and unsettling. The room buzzed with a low murmur as Hancock concluded his presentation, leaving the floor open for questions.

One official, a senior advisor to the Prime Minister, leaned forward, his face etched with worry. "Mr. Hancock, if these texts are accurate, what do you believe the Anunnaki's return signifies for us? Are we facing another era of genetic manipulation and resource extraction?"

Hancock paused, choosing his words carefully. "The texts suggest a cyclical nature to their visits, linked to Nibiru's orbit. If they are indeed returning, it could mean they have unfinished business here, or they need resources that only Earth can provide. It's crucial we prepare for all possibilities, understanding their past intentions to anticipate their future actions."

The room fell silent as the weight of his words settled in. The revelation was not just about the scientific marvel of a rogue planet, but about the potential return of beings who had once shaped the course of human history. Hancock's insights provided a bridge between ancient wisdom and modern crisis management, offering a roadmap for the challenges ahead.

Hancock meticulously laid out the evidence, showing slides of cuneiform tablets and translating the ancient symbols with a practiced fluency that captivated his audience. The room dimmed as the projector cast images of the aged, clay tablets onto the wall, each one a relic from a bygone era. Hancock's voice, steady and authoritative, guided them through the intricate details etched into these ancient artifacts.

"The Sumerian texts," he began, "detail the arrival of the Anunnaki, a race of advanced beings from Nibiru. These texts are not mere myths, but historical accounts written by the scribes of ancient Mesopotamia." As he spoke, he highlighted specific passages, translating the symbols into English. The audience watched in rapt silence, the air thick with tension and awe, as he revealed the narrative of these celestial visitors.

According to the texts, the Anunnaki descended upon Earth with a clear purpose: to extract gold. This precious metal was not just a luxury for them but a necessity, vital for the survival of their home planet, Nibiru. Their quest for gold led them to undertake genetic experiments on early humans, creating a labor force capable of performing the arduous task of mining. Hancock showed slides of detailed illustrations and annotations, ancient records that described these genetic manipulations with surprising clarity.

"Their impact on human civilization was profound," Hancock continued, his tone somber. "The Anunnaki's intervention accelerated the development of early societies, introducing advanced knowledge and techniques that seemed almost miraculous to our ancestors." He pointed to depictions of complex technologies and structures that appeared far beyond the capabilities of the time, attributing these advancements to the influence of the Anunnaki.

As he connected the dots between ancient myths and modern science, the room's atmosphere grew even more charged. Hancock suggested that the return of Nibiru could signal the return of the Anunnaki, a concept that resonated deeply with his audience. "This isn't just an astronomical event," he emphasized, "but potentially a re-enactment of a cosmic cycle described in ancient lore."

The implications were staggering, blending the boundaries between history, mythology, and reality. Hancock's evidence suggested that humanity was not only facing a celestial phenomenon but also the possible return of beings who had once shaped the very foundations of human civilization. The slides continued to flash, each one a piece of the puzzle that painted a picture of a world on the brink of a new chapter.

Hancock's presentation concluded with a somber note. "We must prepare," he warned, "not just for a celestial encounter, but for the possible return of these ancient visitors. Their motives, their intentions—these are questions we need to answer swiftly and accurately." He paused, letting the gravity of his words settle in. "History, mythology, and reality are converging. We stand at the threshold of an epochal moment, and it is imperative that we approach it with knowledge, caution, and unity."

The room remained silent as Hancock stepped back, the weight of his revelations hanging heavily in the air. The officials and scientists, once skeptical, now shared a collective understanding of the magnitude of the situation. The blending of ancient history with impending reality had transformed their perspective, highlighting the urgent need for preparedness and collaboration.

As the lights came back on, the discussion began in earnest. Plans were made to further investigate the historical accounts, to seek out additional texts and artifacts that might provide more insight into the Anunnaki and their intentions. Scientists discussed the implications for their fields, considering how this new information might influence their approach to studying Nibiru.

Hancock's presentation had not just informed but galvanized the room. The blend of historical evidence and modern science had forged a new path forward, one that acknowledged the lessons of the past while preparing for the uncertainties of the future. As the meeting adjourned, there was a palpable sense of resolve. Humanity would face this challenge head-on, armed with the knowledge of ancient warnings and the determination to navigate the cosmic convergence that lay ahead.

Meanwhile, Jordan Peterson was summoned to another meeting, this one convened in a fortified conference room within a government complex, the walls lined with screens displaying real-time data and news feeds. Present were world leaders, top psychologists, and high-ranking officials from international health organizations. The growing panic among the global population required immediate attention, and Peterson, with his deep understanding of mythology and human psychology, was the ideal candidate to advise on managing the situation.

Peterson's reputation for blending analytical rigor with empathetic insight made him a natural choice. He understood that such an unprecedented event as the approach of Nibiru would awaken primal fears buried deep within the human psyche. As he entered the room, the atmosphere was thick with tension, the faces of the assembled dignitaries reflecting a mix of anxiety and anticipation.

Taking his place at the head of the table, Peterson began his address. He emphasized the importance of clear communication and psychological support, stressing that misinformation and fear could spread faster than any physical impact of the celestial event. His voice was calm and measured, a stark contrast to the turmoil outside the conference room.

"Throughout history," Peterson began, "humankind has faced numerous cataclysmic events, many of which have been enshrined in our myths and legends. These stories, while sometimes dramatized, reflect real human experiences and responses to existential threats." He drew parallels between ancient myths of floods, fires, and cosmic upheavals and the current crisis. "These narratives have served as tools for our ancestors to make sense of the world, to frame their fears within a context that emphasizes survival and adaptation."

Peterson's approach was both analytical and empathetic. He recognized the deep-seated fears that Nibiru's approach had triggered, but he also saw an opportunity to harness these fears productively. By framing Nibiru's approach within a broader narrative of human resilience and adaptability, Peterson aimed to provide a sense of control and hope. "We must remember that our species has endured and thrived through countless challenges. This crisis, like those before it, can be navigated with wisdom, courage, and unity."

He advocated for the use of structured routines to maintain a sense of normalcy. "Daily routines provide stability and predictability, which are crucial in times of uncertainty. Encourage people to stick to their schedules, to engage in familiar activities. This can help mitigate the sense of chaos and keep anxiety at bay."

Furthermore, Peterson stressed the importance of community support. "Isolation can exacerbate fear. It is vital to foster a sense of community, whether through physical gatherings where safe, or virtual connections. People need to know they are not alone, that their concerns are shared, and that support is available."

He also suggested practical measures, such as setting up helplines staffed by mental health professionals, creating online forums for community support, and ensuring that accurate information was readily available to counteract rumors and misinformation. "Effective communication is key," he noted. "Leaders must be transparent about what is known and what remains uncertain. Providing regular updates can help build trust and reduce the spread of panic."

Peterson's message was clear and actionable. He offered a blend of psychological insight and practical advice, aiming to equip the leaders with tools to manage the public's response effectively. His emphasis on framing the crisis within a narrative of human resilience resonated deeply, offering a counterbalance to the pervasive fear.

As the meeting progressed, world leaders and psychologists discussed how to implement Peterson's recommendations. Plans were made to launch public information campaigns, establish mental health support networks, and promote community engagement initiatives. Peterson's insights provided a roadmap for navigating the psychological landscape of the crisis, transforming fear into a catalyst for unity and strength.

By the end of the meeting, there was a renewed sense of purpose among the participants. Peterson's guidance had not only addressed the immediate need for psychological support but had also laid the groundwork for a resilient, informed public. The strategies discussed would be rolled out globally, aiming to stabilize societies and prepare them for the challenges ahead.

Peterson left the meeting with a sense of accomplishment, knowing that his expertise would help steer humanity through the turbulent times to come. His role, like Hancock's, was crucial in ensuring that the world faced the impending encounter with Nibiru not with despair, but with a fortified spirit and a collective resolve to overcome future tribulations.

As the meetings progressed, it became increasingly clear that Hancock and Peterson's insights complemented each other perfectly. Hancock's extensive knowledge of ancient civilizations and their texts provided a tangible framework for understanding humanity's past encounters with celestial phenomena. He painted vivid pictures of ancient societies grappling with otherworldly visitors, their responses documented in myths and legends that had survived millennia. This historical context was invaluable, offering a narrative continuity that helped make sense of the current crisis.

Peterson, on the other hand, brought to the table his deep understanding of human psychology and behavior. His expertise in addressing existential fears and maintaining mental health offered crucial strategies for coping with the present and preparing for the future. He recognized the primal fears evoked by Nibiru's approach and knew how to channel these anxieties into constructive actions. His approach was grounded in empathy and pragmatism, focusing on resilience and adaptability.

The two men were introduced in a high-level meeting, and

despite their different backgrounds—one a historian and the other a psychologist—they quickly recognized the immense value in working together. Their mutual respect was immediate, each seeing in the other the missing piece needed to address the multifaceted challenges posed by Nibiru. They formed an unlikely but powerful alliance, pooling their knowledge and resources to craft a comprehensive plan to prepare humanity for what was to come.

Hancock committed to continuing his deep dive into ancient texts, seeking further clues about the Anunnaki and their intentions. He scoured through every available artifact, tablet, and manuscript, driven by a sense of urgency. His research became more collaborative, involving linguists, archaeologists, and even astrophysicists, aiming to decode every possible piece of information. He organized symposiums and workshops, sharing his findings with a broader audience of scholars and encouraging a multidisciplinary approach to understanding the historical significance of Nibiru's return.

Peterson, meanwhile, focused on developing psychological support systems and public communication strategies. He worked closely with mental health professionals to create resources that would be accessible to people worldwide. He spearheaded initiatives to train community leaders and volunteers in providing psychological first aid, recognizing the importance of grassroots support in maintaining societal stability. His public addresses, broadcast through various media channels, aimed to calm fears and foster a sense of collective resilience.

Together, their combined efforts aimed to bridge the gap between historical understanding and contemporary coping mechanisms. They co-authored articles and conducted joint presentations, seamlessly integrating Hancock's historical insights with Peterson's psychological strategies. Their collaboration extended to advising governments and international organizations, ensuring that policies and emergency plans were informed by both the lessons of the past and the realities of human psychology.

Their plan was multifaceted, addressing both the intellectual and emotional needs of the global population. Hancock's historical context gave people a sense of continuity, showing that humanity had faced and survived similar challenges before. Peterson's psychological strategies provided practical tools for coping with fear and uncertainty, emphasizing the importance of community and resilience.

As their alliance strengthened, so did the world's preparedness. The narrative they constructed, one of informed understanding and proactive mental health support, began to permeate public consciousness. Schools incorporated lessons from Hancock's findings into their curricula, teaching children about ancient civilizations and the importance of historical knowledge. Mental health campaigns, inspired by Peterson's guidance, promoted well-being and community support.

Hancock and Peterson's collaboration became a beacon of hope and rationality in an otherwise chaotic time. Their efforts not only prepared humanity for the impending celestial encounter but also fostered a renewed appreciation for the interconnectedness of history and psychology. By bridging these two domains, they provided a holistic approach to facing the unknown, ensuring that humanity would not only survive but thrive in the face of the extraordinary challenges ahead.

With their roles clearly defined, Hancock and Peterson set to work with a sense of urgency and purpose. Hancock returned to his study, his sanctuary of ancient wisdom, and immersed himself in the labyrinthine depths of old manuscripts and tablets. His study, already overflowing with historical treasures, became a hive of activity. Bookshelves groaned under the weight of ancient texts, and his desk was cluttered with scrolls, maps, and artifacts from various epochs. The faint scent of aged paper and ink filled the air, a testament to the centuries of knowledge contained within these walls.

Hancock reached out to fellow historians and archaeologists, forming an unprecedented network dedicated to uncovering every possible detail about the Anunnaki and Nibiru. This coalition of scholars spanned continents, linked by a shared mission and the latest in digital communication technology. They held virtual conferences, exchanged emails brimming with new insights, and even conducted joint field expeditions to uncover more artifacts. Their collaborative spirit was invigorating, each discovery propelling them forward.

The findings were compiled into comprehensive reports, meticulously detailing the historical accounts and their potential implications for the present. These reports, filled with translated texts, comparative analyses, and cross-referenced historical data, were shared with governments and scientific bodies worldwide. Hancock's team produced multimedia presentations and detailed dossiers that were used in policy-making, scientific research, and public education. The historical narrative of the Anunnaki and their previous visits to Earth provided a crucial context for understanding the present situation.

Peterson, on the other hand, focused on the human element with equal vigor. He conducted workshops and seminars, both online and in-person, training mental health professionals to address the unique psychological challenges posed by the impending event. His sessions were comprehensive, covering topics from basic stress management techniques to more complex strategies for community-wide psychological resilience. He developed training modules that were distributed globally, ensuring that even the most remote communities had access to vital mental health resources.

Appearing on television and social media, Peterson became a familiar and reassuring presence. His calm demeanor and clear, practical advice helped to soothe the public's anxieties. He spoke about the importance of maintaining routines, fostering connections with loved ones, and staying informed through reliable sources. He encouraged people to find strength in community and shared humanity, emphasizing that collective resilience was the key to overcoming the psychological impact of Nibiru's approach.

Peterson's efforts extended to creating support networks that could operate at the grassroots level. Community leaders were trained to recognize signs of psychological distress and to provide basic support until professional help could be accessed. Online forums and hotlines were established, offering anonymous counseling and advice. These initiatives created a safety net for millions, ensuring that help was available to anyone in need.

As Nibiru drew ever closer, the world watched and waited, but this time with a sense of preparedness that had not been present before. The pervasive fear that had once gripped humanity was now tempered by a structured approach to both the historical and psychological aspects of the crisis. Thanks to the combined efforts of Hancock and Peterson, humanity was not facing the unknown blindly. They had a historical context that provided insight into the possible motivations and actions of the Anunnaki, and a psychological framework that equipped them to handle the emotional and mental challenges.

The stage was set for an unprecedented encounter, one that would forever alter the course of human history. But this time, there was a glimmer of hope. The understanding and unity fostered by Hancock and Peterson's collaboration had lit a way forward. Governments were better prepared to make informed decisions, scientists were ready to study and mitigate the physical impacts, and communities were fortified by psychological resilience and mutual support.

In the midst of uncertainty, humanity found strength in knowledge and solidarity. The anticipation of Nibiru's arrival was no longer solely a source of dread but also an opportunity to demonstrate human ingenuity, cooperation, and resilience. The world stood on the brink of a new era, ready to face the challenges and opportunities that the future would bring, united in purpose and fortified by the wisdom of the past and the strength of their shared humanity.

CHAPTER 3: THE APPROACH

As Nibiru drew closer, the world watched with bated breath. What had once been a distant and almost mythical object of speculation was now an undeniable reality, commanding the attention of every corner of the globe. By early 2029, Nibiru had become visible to the naked eye, a colossal, reddish orb that loomed ominously in the night sky. Its appearance was both mesmerizing and terrifying, an unblinking eye in the heavens that served as a constant reminder of the unknown fate awaiting humanity.

The planet's reddish hue seemed to pulse with a life of its own, casting a faint, eerie glow over the landscape. People across the globe gathered in parks, on rooftops, and in backyards, their faces upturned in a mix of fear and fascination. Conversations hushed as the celestial visitor made its nightly appearance, its presence a silent testament to the cosmic forces at play. Amateur astronomers and curious onlookers set up telescopes, sharing views and theories, as the presence of Nibiru became an integral part of daily life. In cities and towns, makeshift observation parties sprang up, complete with lawn chairs, blankets, and hot beverages, as communities came together to witness the extraordinary sight.

News outlets provided constant coverage, tracking Nibiru's approach with an urgency usually reserved for natural disasters and breaking news of monumental significance. Television networks aired special segments, featuring expert panels and detailed simulations of the planet's trajectory. Journalists reported from observatories and research centers, bringing the latest updates directly to the public. The planet's ominous approach dominated headlines, pushing other news stories to the margins. Newspapers ran front-page stories with titles like "The Countdown to Nibiru" and "The Celestial Intruder."

Social media buzzed with updates, photographs, and videos, each post fueling the worldwide conversation. Hashtags like #NibiruWatch and #CosmicCountdown trended globally, as people shared their personal experiences and observations. Some posts were filled with scientific curiosity, others with existential dread, but all contributed to a sense of global community grappling with an unprecedented event. Influencers and celebrities weighed in, some posting inspirational messages of unity and hope, others sharing their own anxieties about the future.

The scientific community worked tirelessly, refining models and predictions to understand the rogue planet's trajectory and possible effects on Earth. Laboratories and observatories operated around the clock, their efforts coordinated through international networks and collaborations. Teams of astronomers, physicists, and engineers pored over data, adjusting their calculations with each new piece of information. Supercomputers ran continuous simulations, mapping out potential scenarios and their implications.

Specialized research teams delved into historical records, cross-referencing ancient texts and astronomical logs in an attempt to glean any clues from humanity's past encounters with celestial phenomena. The integration of modern technology with ancient knowledge painted a picture that was both complex and fascinating, suggesting that humanity had always been under the watchful gaze of the cosmos. Conferences and symposiums were held, where experts shared their findings and debated the best course of action.

The atmosphere was charged with anticipation and unease, a

global collective holding its breath as the celestial body edged closer. Families prepared emergency kits, governments issued guidelines, and schools held special assemblies to discuss Nibiru's significance. Artists and writers found inspiration in the planet's approach, producing works that captured the blend of awe and fear permeating society. The world was united in its vigilant watch, every eye turned skyward in a mix of hope, dread, and wonder.

In this charged environment, humanity's ingenuity and resilience shone through. Despite the pervasive sense of uncertainty, there was also a burgeoning sense of solidarity. Communities banded together, sharing resources and supporting one another. Science and art intertwined, as the need to understand and the need to express became equally important. As Nibiru loomed ever larger, the world prepared itself not just for the potential impacts of a rogue planet, but for a profound encounter with the unknown.

Elon Musk, ever the visionary and driven by his insatiable curiosity, saw an unprecedented opportunity in the approaching celestial event. As the founder of multiple groundbreaking companies and a relentless advocate for space exploration, Musk was known for his ambitious projects and bold ideas. The sight of Nibiru in the sky, with its potential to forever alter the course of human history, sparked in him a daring plan: to establish contact with the Anunnaki and seek their advanced technology.

Musk envisioned a future where humanity could leverage the knowledge of these ancient visitors to accelerate his mission to colonize Mars and secure humanity's future among the stars. The potential benefits were immense: the Anunnaki, if they indeed possessed the technological prowess described in ancient texts, could provide insights into sustainable energy, efficient space travel, and even groundbreaking medical advancements. Musk believed that their advanced technology could solve many of Earth's most pressing problems and propel humanity into a new era of exploration and innovation.

His proposal, however, was met with a mix of skepticism and intrigue from the global community. Critics questioned the feasibility of contacting extraterrestrial beings based on ancient myths, while others feared the potential risks of such an endeavor. Despite the doubts, Musk remained undeterred. He was convinced that the rewards far outweighed the risks and that the current crisis demanded extraordinary measures.

Determined to gain support, Musk presented his plan to world leaders and scientific advisors at a high-stakes international summit. The room was filled with the most influential minds in politics, science, and technology, all eager to hear what the maverick entrepreneur had to say. Musk took the stage with his characteristic confidence, his eyes alight with the fire of innovation.

He began by outlining the historical context, referencing the Sumerian texts that spoke of the Anunnaki and their previous visits to Earth. Musk highlighted the technological advancements attributed to these beings, suggesting that their influence had once propelled human civilization forward. He argued that reconnecting with the Anunnaki could once again spark a renaissance of technological and scientific progress.

Musk's arguments were compelling. He spoke passionately about the potential benefits of such an encounter, emphasizing how the Anunnaki's advanced technology could revolutionize sustainable energy, making it possible to power the world cleanly and efficiently. He described how their knowledge of space travel could unlock new methods of propulsion, enabling faster and safer journeys to Mars and beyond. Musk even touched on the possibility of medical breakthroughs, hinting at cures for diseases that had plagued humanity for centuries.

"The meeting with the Anunnaki," Musk asserted, "is not just a chance to learn; it is a necessity for humanity's survival and progress. We stand at a crossroads. The challenges we face today require solutions that lie beyond our current technological capabilities. By reaching out to beings who may have once shaped our civilization, we can gain the tools we need to secure a brighter future for all of humanity."

He painted a vivid picture of a future where humans and Anunnaki worked together to explore the cosmos, share knowledge, and build a sustainable, thriving interplanetary society. The idea of reaching out to beings who might have once shaped human civilization added an element of historical significance to his proposal. It was not just about technological gain but also about reclaiming a lost part of human heritage and identity.

Musk's presentation sparked vigorous debate among the attendees. Some were deeply moved by his vision and the possibilities it presented, while others remained cautious, concerned about the unknown risks. Yet, as the discussions unfolded, it became clear that the urgency of the situation required bold and innovative thinking. The prospect of establishing contact with the Anunnaki and harnessing their advanced technology became a beacon of hope in a time of unprecedented uncertainty.

Ultimately, the global community began to rally behind Musk's proposal. Governments, scientific institutions, and private organizations pledged their support, pooling resources and expertise to prepare for the historic encounter. Musk's unwavering belief in the potential of human ingenuity and his fearless pursuit of knowledge had once again inspired the world to reach for the stars. As preparations commenced, the anticipation of what lay ahead infused humanity with a renewed sense of purpose and determination.

The governments of the world, after much deliberation and consultation with their scientific communities, ultimately agreed to Musk's proposal. The potential benefits of establishing contact with the Anunnaki far outweighed the risks, and the urgency of the situation demanded bold action. Recognizing the historic significance and the high stakes involved, they decided that a coordinated, international effort was necessary to ensure the mission's success and humanity's safety.

An international task force was formed, comprising leading scientists, diplomats, and security experts from various nations. This elite group was tasked with overseeing the preparations for the historic encounter, their work carried out under strict confidentiality to prevent public panic and ensure the operation remained secure. The task force operated with a level of secrecy akin to the highest military operations, understanding that the potential for misinformation or sabotage was high.

Preparations were meticulous and multifaceted, leaving no stone unturned. Communication protocols were at the forefront of these efforts. Linguists, cryptographers, and AI specialists collaborated to develop a universal message that could be understood by an advanced extraterrestrial race. They used both human intellect and artificial intelligence to create a complex yet comprehensible communication system, blending mathematical principles with universal scientific concepts.

Contingency plans were developed for every conceivable scenario, from peaceful exchange to defensive measures. The task force worked through exhaustive simulations and drills, preparing for outcomes ranging from a cordial alliance to hostile encounters. Military units were placed on high alert, their roles clearly defined in the event of any aggressive moves by the Anunnaki. Diplomatic teams crafted negotiation strategies, studying historical precedents and extraterrestrial communication theories to be as prepared as possible.

The logistics of the meeting were complex, involving the coordination of space agencies, military units, and scientific institutions from around the globe. Space agencies like NASA, ESA, and Roscosmos collaborated closely, pooling their resources and expertise. Advanced satellites and telescopes were aligned to monitor Nibiru and the Anunnaki's approach, while spacefaring nations readied their fleets for potential space rendezvous.

Military units, including elite special forces and defense specialists, were discreetly mobilized, ensuring that the encounter site was secure and that all defensive measures were in place. Scientific institutions contributed their best minds, focusing on areas such as extraterrestrial biology, physics, and engineering, to provide real-time analysis and support during the encounter.

The chosen meeting site was a remote, secure location, selected for its strategic advantages and ability to host the necessary technological infrastructure. Engineers and architects designed and constructed a state-of-the-art facility equipped with advanced communication equipment, research laboratories, and security systems. This facility became the nerve center for the operation, where the task force would monitor every aspect of the encounter in real-time.

In parallel, public information campaigns were carefully crafted, ready to be deployed at the appropriate time. These campaigns aimed to manage the eventual disclosure of the mission, balancing transparency with the need to maintain public order. Psychologists and sociologists were consulted to ensure the messages would be effective in mitigating panic and fostering a sense of global unity and preparedness.

As the days turned into weeks and the preparations neared completion, a sense of unprecedented anticipation hung in the air. The task force, now a well-oiled machine, was ready to implement their plans at a moment's notice. The combined efforts of scientists, diplomats, and military personnel had created a robust framework designed to handle any situation that might arise during the encounter.

In this atmosphere of cautious optimism, humanity prepared to reach out and touch the unknown, ready to face the potential for profound change. The world held its breath, united in hope and determination, as the stage was set for a moment that would forever alter the course of human history.

As the preparations progressed, the anticipation built to a fever pitch. The public, acutely aware that something monumental was in the works but left in the dark about the specifics, speculated endlessly. Conversations in cafes, offices, and online forums buzzed with theories and conjectures. Rumors and leaks only added to the growing sense of expectancy, with each new tidbit of information igniting fresh waves of excitement and anxiety.

Media outlets reported on the buildup with fervor, piecing together fragments of information from unnamed sources and interviewing experts who could offer only educated guesses. Evening news segments and special reports were dedicated to Nibiru and the forthcoming encounter, featuring dramatic headlines and eye-catching graphics. Documentaries exploring the myths of the Anunnaki and the scientific implications of extraterrestrial contact surged in popularity. The global conversation was dominated by Nibiru and the potential for contact, eclipsing all other news stories.

Elon Musk, at the forefront of the mission, became a symbol of humanity's hopeful and adventurous spirit. His public appearances were highly anticipated events, drawing massive audiences both in person and online. Musk continued to communicate openly with the public, carefully balancing transparency with the need for discretion. His speeches and interviews were filled with optimism, urging people to look to the future with hope and confidence. He spoke of the incredible possibilities that contact with the Anunnaki could unlock, from technological advancements to a deeper understanding of our place in the universe.

His charisma and vision inspired millions, galvanizing support for the mission and fostering a sense of unity and purpose. Social media was awash with hashtags like #MuskMission and

#HopeForHumanity, as people rallied behind the cause. Public opinion, initially divided, began to coalesce around a shared hope for a breakthrough that could change the course of human history.

Meanwhile, the scientific community worked around the clock. Laboratories buzzed with activity, filled with the hum of high-tech equipment and the murmur of intense discussions. Research teams cross-referenced historical texts, astronomical data, and advanced simulations, striving to piece together a comprehensive understanding of Nibiru and its inhabitants. Experts in fields ranging from genetics to engineering collaborated seamlessly, their collective effort pushing the boundaries of human knowledge.

Psychologists and sociologists played a crucial role, studying the potential cultural impacts of contact with the Anunnaki. They developed strategies to help societies integrate any new knowledge smoothly, minimizing disruption and fostering acceptance. Workshops and seminars were conducted to prepare educators, community leaders, and policymakers for the potential changes ahead. The focus was on building resilience and adaptability, ensuring that humanity could thrive in the face of unprecedented challenges and opportunities.

The collective effort was a testament to humanity's ingenuity and determination in the face of the unknown. It showcased the best of what humans could achieve when united by a common goal. The tireless work of scientists, engineers, diplomats, and countless others created a robust framework designed to handle any scenario that might arise from the encounter.

As the day of the encounter approached, a palpable sense of anticipation gripped the world. The night skies, dominated by the looming presence of Nibiru, became a nightly reminder of the historic moment drawing closer. Schools held special assemblies, workplaces organized viewing events, and families made plans to gather together. There was an undercurrent of hope that transcended borders and cultures, a shared belief that humanity stood on the brink of something extraordinary.

In this atmosphere of eager expectancy, humanity prepared to reach out to the stars, ready to embrace whatever the future might hold. The collective will to understand and explore had never been stronger. With Musk as their figurehead and the scientific community as their backbone, people around the globe braced for an encounter that would forever alter their understanding of the universe and their place within it.

Finally, the day of the historic encounter arrived. The chosen site was a remote and secure location, a hidden valley nestled deep within the mountains, carefully selected to minimize risks and ensure privacy. Security was tight, with multiple layers of defense to protect against any unforeseen threats. The area had been declared a no-fly zone, and access was strictly controlled, ensuring that only authorized personnel were present.

A specially designed facility had been constructed at the site, blending cutting-edge technology with meticulous planning. The facility was equipped with the latest communication devices, capable of transmitting and receiving signals across vast distances and even different dimensions, should the need arise. Advanced holographic projectors were in place to facilitate visual communication, and translation algorithms had been integrated to bridge any language barriers. Every detail had been considered, from the acoustics of the meeting room to the environmental controls that would ensure a comfortable atmosphere for all participants.

The task force, led by Musk, was in place, ready to make contact with beings who had once walked the Earth. Specialists from various fields, including linguistics, anthropology, and quantum physics, stood by, each prepared to contribute their expertise to the historic meeting. Musk himself was a figure of calm determination, his eyes reflecting the weight of the moment and the anticipation of what was to come.

The atmosphere was electric with anticipation. As Nibiru hovered closer, its details visible even without telescopes, the moment felt surreal. The planet's surface, with its swirling patterns and mysterious landscapes, was now clearly discernible, capturing the imagination of everyone who beheld it. The sky was a tapestry of celestial grandeur, dominated by the looming presence of the rogue planet, casting a soft, eerie light over the facility and its surroundings.

Humanity stood on the brink of a new era, poised to reach out and touch the unknown. The collective hope and anxiety of billions of people were palpable, a global heartbeat synchronized in anticipation. As the appointed time approached, a hush fell over the facility. Every eye was turned skyward, every breath held in suspense.

Then, breaking the stillness, a point of light appeared in the sky, growing steadily brighter. As it descended, its shape became clearer, revealing a ship unlike any earthly craft. The Anunnaki's vessel shimmered with an otherworldly light, its surface smooth and seamless, reflecting the surrounding landscape like a mirror. It moved with a grace and precision that defied human engineering, descending slowly and silently until it hovered just above the ground.

The world held its breath. The culmination of years of preparation and millennia of myth and history was at hand. Every screen, from the monitors in the facility to televisions and mobile devices around the globe, broadcast the moment live. The collective gaze of humanity was fixed on this single point of contact, this bridge between worlds.

The ship's descent was marked by a gentle hum, a resonance that seemed to touch something deep within the observers. As it settled, a ramp extended from its side, and a figure emerged, bathed in the same ethereal light that surrounded the vessel. The Anunnaki had arrived.

The stage was set for an encounter that would forever alter

the course of human history. Musk and the task force stepped forward, ready to initiate the first contact. The air was thick with anticipation and hope, a shared belief that understanding and unity could light the way forward. The ancient myths and modern aspirations converged in this singular moment, a testament to humanity's enduring quest for knowledge and connection.

As Musk extended a hand in greeting, the world watched, united in its desire for peace and enlightenment. This was the dawn of a new chapter, one that promised to unlock the secrets of the cosmos and redefine humanity's place within it. The hope was that this encounter would not only yield technological advancements but also foster a deeper understanding of our shared history and potential future. The Anunnaki's return was not just an end but a beginning, a chance to build a future guided by the lessons of the past and the aspirations of the present.

CHAPTER 4: THE ARRIVAL

In 2030, Nibiru crossed Earth's orbit, marking a momentous event in human history. This celestial body, shrouded in mystery and myth, had been the subject of intense speculation and scientific scrutiny for years. The rogue planet's passage through the solar system had been anticipated with a mixture of fear, awe, and scientific curiosity. As Nibiru loomed closer, its gravitational effects were felt across Earth, causing subtle yet noticeable shifts in weather patterns and tides. Coastal areas experienced higher tides, while unusual weather phenomena were reported globally, ranging from unseasonal storms to changes in temperature. Seismologists noted a slight increase in tectonic activity, attributing it to the gravitational pull of the massive planet.

The world watched with bated breath as telescopes and satellites captured every detail of the planet's journey. Major observatories streamed live feeds, and amateur astronomers shared their own footage, creating a global tapestry of observations. The night skies were dominated by the sight of Nibiru, its reddish hue casting an eerie glow. Public interest soared, with people gathering in open spaces to witness the celestial spectacle. Educational programs on television and the internet explained the science behind Nibiru, while historians delved into the myths and legends associated with it.

Then, as if scripted by the cosmos itself, the Anunnaki made contact. The anticipation that had gripped humanity reached a fever pitch. Their ships descended from the sky, sleek and shimmering, moving with a grace that defied the known laws of physics. Observers described the ships as ethereal, almost dreamlike, their surfaces reflecting the surrounding landscape like liquid mirrors. They moved silently, effortlessly, a testament to the advanced technology of their creators. No engines roared, no exhaust plumes marred the air; they simply glided, as if on invisible rails.

The chosen landing site was the same remote facility where preparations had been meticulously carried out. This site, chosen for its seclusion and security, had been equipped with the latest technology and fortified to ensure the safety of all involved. As the first ship touched down, a hush fell over the world. Every screen, from smartphones to giant public displays, broadcasted the moment live. The ramp extended, and three figures emerged, each radiating an aura of authority and otherworldly presence.

Leading them was Lord Enki, the geneticist who had designed humanity. Enki's presence was commanding yet inviting, his eyes reflecting centuries of wisdom and curiosity. His attire, a blend of ancient regalia and futuristic design, hinted at his dual role as a scientist and a leader. Beside him was his brother, Lord Enlil, a stern and imposing military leader. Enlil's demeanor was one of steely resolve, his posture and expression exuding discipline and authority. His armor-like garments shimmered with an inner light, symbolizing his role as a protector and enforcer of Anunnaki law.

Accompanying them was Inanna, a being of unparalleled beauty and grace, her presence commanding both respect and admiration. Inanna's movements were fluid, almost ethereal, and her attire was adorned with intricate patterns that seemed to shift and change as she moved. Her eyes, deep and luminous, captivated everyone who looked upon her. She embodied both the nurturing aspects of a deity and the fierce independence of a warrior.

The arrival of the Anunnaki was a sight to behold, a convergence of ancient mythology and modern reality. As the world held its breath, these celestial visitors took their first steps on Earth in millennia, their return marking the beginning of a new chapter in human history. The initial awe and reverence were palpable, as humanity stood on the brink of an unprecedented encounter, ready to embrace the unknown and forge a future shaped by interstellar collaboration.

The task force, led by Elon Musk, approached the Anunnaki with a mixture of reverence and cautious optimism. The air was thick with anticipation and the weight of historical significance. Musk, known for his audacity and vision, was now the face of humanity in this unprecedented encounter. His usual confidence was tempered with a deep sense of responsibility, his eyes reflecting the hopes and fears of billions.

Alongside him were key figures such as Jordan Peterson, who had been instrumental in preparing the psychological framework for this moment. Peterson's calm demeanor and intellectual gravitas were invaluable in setting a tone of thoughtful engagement. Other representatives from the international community, including diplomats, scientists, and cultural leaders, stood by, each selected for their expertise and their ability to contribute to the dialogue that was about to unfold.

As the task force approached, Enki stepped forward, his presence both commanding and serene. His eyes, deep and knowing, scanned the humans with a mixture of curiosity and recognition. He seemed to assess them not just as individuals, but as representatives of an entire species. His gaze lingered on Musk and Peterson, sensing the intellectual and philosophical kinship they shared. It was as if he could see into their minds, recognizing their potential as partners in the journey of discovery and advancement.

Through a series of gestures and the use of advanced

translation devices, the Anunnaki initiated communication. Their language, a blend of harmonic tones and intricate symbols, was quickly decoded by the AI systems that had been meticulously prepared for this moment. The harmonic tones resonated through the air, creating a melodic yet deeply meaningful dialogue, while the symbols appeared as holographic projections, adding a visual layer to their communication.

Enki spoke first, his voice resonant and calm, carrying an authority that demanded attention. "We have returned," he said, his words echoing through the minds of those present, amplified by the translation devices to ensure clarity. The statement hung in the air, heavy with the implications of their shared history. "Our history with your kind is long and complex. We come not as conquerors, but as allies. There is much we can learn from each other."

The declaration was met with a wave of relief and excitement. Musk stepped forward, his voice steady but charged with emotion. "Welcome back to Earth," he said, extending a hand in a gesture of goodwill. "We have much to share and even more to learn. Let us build a future together, one that honors our past and looks forward to new horizons."

Peterson followed, his tone reflective and thoughtful. "This encounter is a profound opportunity for mutual understanding and growth. Our myths and histories have long spoken of your presence. Now, we stand ready to engage in a dialogue that bridges our worlds."

Enki nodded, his expression thoughtful. "Indeed. Our time apart has been long, but it has also allowed both our civilizations to evolve. We bring knowledge and technology, but we also seek to understand how you have grown and what you have discovered."

The conversation flowed, facilitated by the advanced translation devices. The task force and the Anunnaki exchanged information on various topics, from technological advancements and scientific discoveries to cultural achievements and philosophical ideas. The AI systems worked tirelessly, ensuring that every nuance of the complex dialogue was accurately conveyed.

As the initial meeting progressed, the atmosphere shifted from cautious optimism to genuine collaboration. The Anunnaki shared insights into their advanced technologies, revealing potential solutions to some of Earth's most pressing challenges, such as energy sustainability and medical breakthroughs. In return, the humans showcased their own achievements, highlighting the resilience and creativity that had driven their progress.

The presence of the Anunnaki, with their vast knowledge and experience, was both humbling and inspiring. They were beings of great wisdom, yet they approached the encounter with a sense of humility and a genuine desire for mutual benefit. This set the tone for a relationship based on respect and shared goals, laying the groundwork for a partnership that promised to unlock new potentials for both civilizations.

As the day drew to a close, the first steps towards a new era of interstellar collaboration had been taken. The task force, led by Musk and supported by visionaries like Peterson, had successfully initiated a dialogue that held the promise of transforming humanity's future. The Anunnaki, once distant figures of myth and legend, were now partners in a journey towards knowledge, understanding, and progress. The world watched with bated breath, ready to embrace the changes that were sure to come.

The Anunnaki were fascinated by Earth's technological advancements and the preserved knowledge of their history. Their tour of the facility was a journey through time and innovation, showcasing humanity's progress and reverence for its own past. As they moved through the halls, their curiosity and admiration were palpable, each new discovery adding to their appreciation of human ingenuity.

Enki, with his keen scientific mind, was particularly captivated by the strides humanity had made in fields such as genetics and artificial intelligence. He marveled at the quantum computers, sleek and humming with the potential to solve problems once thought insurmountable. Enki's eyes sparkled with intrigue as he engaged in deep conversations with scientists and engineers. They discussed CRISPR gene-editing technologies, artificial neural networks, and the possibilities of machine learning. Enki absorbed their knowledge eagerly, sharing insights from his own vast experience, including advanced Anunnaki techniques in genetic manipulation and bioengineering. His exchanges were not merely academic; they were a blending of ancient wisdom and cutting-edge science, sparking ideas that could lead to groundbreaking innovations.

Inanna, meanwhile, immersed herself in the exploration of human art and culture. Her grace and beauty captivated everyone she met, drawing them into conversations about the essence of creativity and expression. She visited a special exhibition that showcased everything from classical paintings to modern digital art. Each piece told a story of human emotion, struggle, and triumph. Inanna moved from one artwork to another, her eyes reflecting the depth of her engagement. She discussed the symbolism in Renaissance masterpieces, the bold strokes of Impressionist paintings, and the immersive experiences of virtual reality art installations. Inanna seemed genuinely interested in how humanity had used art to capture the soul of its experiences, celebrating both the beauty and the pain of existence. Her presence at the exhibition was not just that of an observer; she was an active participant, sharing stories of Anunnaki art and how their culture expressed the cosmos and the inner self.

Lord Enlil, though more reserved, displayed a keen interest in Earth's military and defense technologies. His stern demeanor softened slightly as he reviewed the strategies, weaponry, and the structure of modern armies. He was particularly impressed by the strategic use of satellite surveillance, drone technology, and cyber warfare tactics. Enlil spent hours in the company of military leaders and defense analysts, comparing contemporary tactics with ancient Anunnaki methods. They discussed the evolution of warfare, the ethical considerations of modern conflict, and the resilience required to defend against both physical and digital threats.

Despite his stern demeanor, Enlil acknowledged the ingenuity and resilience of human defense mechanisms. He appreciated the complexity of integrated defense systems, the precision of guided munitions, and the strategic depth of global military alliances. Enlil shared stories of historic Anunnaki battles, their use of energy-based weapons, and their philosophy of conflict resolution. He recognized the parallels and differences, finding common ground in the shared need for security and protection.

As the tour continued, the Anunnaki's fascination deepened. They explored laboratories where scientists worked on renewable energy sources, marveled at the efficiency of solar panels and wind turbines. They visited medical research facilities, learning about advancements in nanotechnology and personalized medicine. Enki's discussions with biomedical researchers revealed potential collaborations that could revolutionize healthcare.

Inanna attended a concert featuring a symphony orchestra playing both classical and contemporary pieces. She was moved by the power of the music, the way it transcended language and spoke directly to the soul. She later joined a workshop with young artists and musicians, encouraging them to continue their creative pursuits and sharing Anunnaki musical traditions.

Lord Enlil's tour of aerospace facilities included watching a demonstration of a new rocket launch, where he observed the meticulous engineering and teamwork required for space exploration. He compared notes with aerospace engineers on propulsion systems, discussing the feasibility of interstellar travel and the challenges of sustaining life in space.

By the end of their tour, the Anunnaki had gained a profound respect for humanity's achievements. They saw a species capable of remarkable innovation, creativity, and resilience. The exchange of knowledge was not one-sided; it was a mutual enrichment, setting the stage for future collaborations. The Anunnaki's arrival had not only bridged millennia of separation but had also opened new pathways for growth and understanding, heralding an era where ancient wisdom and modern science could coalesce to create a brighter future for both civilizations.

Enki was particularly intrigued by the intellect of Jordan Peterson and Elon Musk, recognizing kindred spirits in their quest for understanding and progress. The initial introductions quickly gave way to deep, meaningful conversations that spanned hours, drawing both humans and Anunnaki into a rich dialogue of ideas and philosophies.

With Jordan Peterson, Enki found a profound connection in their shared interest in the intersections of psychology, mythology, and human development. They explored the symbolic meanings behind ancient myths and their relevance to modern societal structures. Enki shared ancient Anunnaki legends and the psychological principles embedded within them, drawing parallels to human myths from various cultures. Peterson found himself both challenged and inspired by Enki's perspectives. The geneticist's vast knowledge and unique viewpoints offered fresh insights into the archetypal themes that had shaped human consciousness over millennia. They discussed the role of myth in guiding human behavior, the importance of narrative in forming cultural identity, and how these elements influenced the evolution of societies.

Peterson, known for his depth of thought and analytical approach, was invigorated by these discussions. He saw in Enki a mind that could delve into the complexities of the human psyche with a blend of scientific rigor and mythological understanding. This fusion of knowledge allowed Peterson to gain new insights into his own work, broadening his understanding of the human condition and the underlying drivers of societal progress.

With Elon Musk, Enki delved into the intricacies of space travel and colonization, topics close to both their hearts. The two exchanged ideas on propulsion systems, sustainable living in extraterrestrial environments, and the future of humanity as a multi-planetary species. Enki shared knowledge of ancient Anunnaki technologies, revealing details of propulsion systems and energy sources that had been lost even to their own civilization over millennia. Musk, ever the visionary, absorbed this information with keen interest, seeing practical applications for his own projects.

Musk revealed his vision for Mars and beyond, describing his plans for creating sustainable human settlements on other planets. He spoke of the challenges of life support systems, the importance of renewable energy, and the need for advanced propulsion to make interplanetary travel more feasible. Enki listened intently, appreciating Musk's ambitious goals and offering insights from the Anunnaki's own experiences with space colonization. Their dialogue was a blend of technical detail and visionary thinking, each idea building upon the other in a dynamic exchange.

These interactions fostered a deep mutual respect. Enki saw in Musk and Peterson the potential for human advancement, a reflection of the Anunnaki's own values of knowledge and exploration. He recognized in them the same relentless curiosity and drive that had propelled the Anunnaki to great heights. Musk and Peterson, in turn, found in Enki a collaborator who not only understood their ambitions but also shared their commitment to pushing the boundaries of what was possible.

The bond that formed between them was not just intellectual, but also personal, built on a shared commitment to the pursuit of knowledge and the betterment of their respective civilizations. Enki's engagement with Peterson and Musk was characterized by a genuine exchange of ideas, where each party learned from the other and grew in understanding. Their collaboration promised to yield advancements that could benefit both humanity and the Anunnaki, fostering a partnership grounded in mutual respect and shared goals.

As their discussions continued, the potential for joint projects became apparent. Enki proposed collaborative research initiatives that could leverage Anunnaki technology and human ingenuity. Musk and Peterson eagerly agreed, seeing the immense possibilities such cooperation could bring. These initiatives ranged from developing new space travel technologies to exploring the psychological impacts of long-term space habitation.

In Enki, Musk and Peterson found not just an ally, but a mentor and a friend. Their interactions laid the groundwork for a future where human and Anunnaki knowledge could coalesce to create unprecedented advancements. The intellectual and personal bonds they forged heralded a new era of collaboration, one that promised to unlock the mysteries of the universe and propel both civilizations towards a brighter future.

As the initial contact phase concluded, it became clear that the Anunnaki were not merely interested in observing but were eager to collaborate. Their curiosity about humanity's progress was matched by a genuine desire to work together towards mutual goals. The Anunnaki's approach was not condescending or paternalistic; instead, it was characterized by a deep respect for human ingenuity and potential. This mutual respect laid the foundation for a series of ambitious joint ventures.

Plans were set in motion for joint projects that would leverage the strengths of both civilizations. The first step was the formation of interdisciplinary research teams, combining the best minds from both human and Anunnaki societies. These teams were tasked with tackling some of the most pressing challenges facing humanity, from climate change to space exploration. Scientists and engineers from both worlds came together in state-of-the-art laboratories, sharing knowledge and technology. The collaborative spirit was palpable, with each breakthrough celebrated as a collective achievement.

One of the most significant collaborations was in the field of space exploration. The Anunnaki offered to assist in Musk's mission to colonize Mars, introducing him to new propulsion technology far more advanced than anything currently available on Earth. They demonstrated propulsion systems that utilized exotic energy sources, making space travel faster and more efficient. This technology had the potential to reduce travel time to Mars from months to mere weeks, revolutionizing human capability for interplanetary travel.

Additionally, the Anunnaki revealed locations of abandoned facilities on Mars and the Moon. These facilities, remnants of ancient civilizations even older than the Anunnaki, held secrets that could accelerate humanity's efforts to become a multi-planetary species. The structures on Mars were equipped with advanced life support systems and habitats, providing invaluable resources for establishing permanent colonies. On the Moon, ancient processing plants and research stations offered insights into sustainable resource extraction and low-gravity manufacturing.

Enki, always the scientist, shared a groundbreaking revelation: the Moon was a hollow construct of unknown origin, used by the Anunnaki to process gold due to its low gravity. This revelation opened new avenues of research and exploration. Human scientists were intrigued by the implications of such a construct, theorizing about its origins and potential applications for future space infrastructure. Collaborative teams began studying the Moon's interior, hoping to uncover its secrets and adapt its technologies for human use.

The world watched as these collaborations unfolded, filled with a sense of hope and excitement for the future. News of the joint projects spread quickly, capturing the imagination of people everywhere. Documentaries, news segments, and social media buzzed with updates, highlighting the progress and potential of the human-Anunnaki alliance. Public interest in science and space exploration surged, inspiring a new generation of scientists, engineers, and explorers.

The arrival of the Anunnaki marked the beginning of a new era, one where humanity was no longer alone in the cosmos. This newfound companionship brought with it a sense of unity and purpose that transcended national and cultural boundaries. Guided by the hope that understanding and unity could light the way forward, humans and Anunnaki worked together to unlock the mysteries of the universe and build a future defined by knowledge, cooperation, and shared purpose.

Joint research initiatives tackled environmental challenges with a vigor previously unseen. Anunnaki technology was applied to develop new methods for carbon capture, renewable energy production, and ecosystem restoration. These efforts not only mitigated the effects of climate change but also sparked economic growth and job creation in green industries.

In education, exchange programs were established, allowing students and scholars from both civilizations to study and work together. Universities and research institutions hosted Anunnaki lecturers, whose teachings on advanced sciences and ancient wisdom enriched human knowledge. Conversely, human cultural and artistic contributions fascinated the Anunnaki, leading to a vibrant exchange of ideas and creativity.

The economic and cultural benefits of the collaboration were immense. New industries emerged, driven by the technological innovations and scientific discoveries that resulted from the partnership. The global economy experienced a renaissance, characterized by sustainable growth and a focus on scientific and technological advancement. Cultural exchanges fostered a deeper understanding and appreciation of each civilization's heritage, creating a rich tapestry of shared human and Anunnaki experiences.

As the collaborations continued, the bond between humans and Anunnaki grew stronger. This partnership was more than a strategic alliance; it was a testament to the potential of unity and cooperation. Together, they explored the cosmos, unraveling its secrets and expanding the horizons of what was possible. The initial skepticism and fear gave way to a shared vision of a future where knowledge, innovation, and mutual respect paved the way for unprecedented progress.

In this new era, the possibilities seemed limitless. Humanity's dream of reaching the stars was no longer a distant fantasy but a tangible reality, driven by the combined efforts of two civilizations. The legacy of the Anunnaki's return was not just technological and scientific advancement but a profound lesson in the power of collaboration and the boundless potential of a united quest for knowledge and progress.

CHAPTER 5: THE NEGOTIATIONS

The world held its breath as negotiations began. The atmosphere in the grand conference hall was charged with anticipation and a sense of historical significance that was almost palpable. Delegates from every major nation were present, their expressions a mix of hope, anxiety, and determination. Alongside them were leading scientists, engineers, and diplomats, each representing the pinnacle of human achievement in their respective fields. The grand hall itself was a marvel of modern architecture, with high ceilings and walls adorned with intricate artwork that depicted the history of human exploration and discovery.

At the center of the room, representatives of the Anunnaki stood poised and composed, their presence commanding both respect and curiosity. They were tall and elegant, their movements graceful and deliberate. Enki, Lord Enlil, and Inanna were the embodiment of ancient wisdom and advanced technology, their very presence a testament to the fusion of history and futurism. Their attire, a blend of metallic fabrics and organic materials, shimmered under the hall's soft lighting, further emphasizing their otherworldly nature.

The negotiation table, a large circular structure symbolizing unity and equality, was set at the heart of the room. It was designed to foster an atmosphere of collaboration, with no head of the table to imply hierarchy. Holographic displays projected detailed images of Earth, Nibiru, Mars, and the Moon, providing a dynamic and immersive backdrop to the discussions. These images shifted and changed, highlighting key resources, potential project sites, and areas of mutual interest. The advanced technology of the holograms served as a reminder of the stakes and the possibilities that lay ahead.

Elon Musk, as a key figure in the negotiations, sat directly opposite Enki, Lord Enlil, and Inanna, ready to engage in what could be the most important dialogue in human history. Musk's reputation as a visionary and a pioneer in space exploration made him a natural leader for these discussions. His demeanor was one of focused intensity, his eyes reflecting the weight of the moment and the dreams of interplanetary colonization that he had championed for so long.

The Anunnaki began by stating their needs clearly. Enki, with his characteristic calm and clarity, took the lead. His voice, deep and resonant, filled the room as he explained that Nibiru was facing critical shortages of gold and water, resources vital for their survival and technological maintenance. His explanation was accompanied by holographic visuals illustrating Nibiru's environment and the pressing need for these resources. The Earth's abundance of gold and water made it an ideal partner in their quest for sustainability.

In exchange, the Anunnaki offered technological advancements that could propel humanity into a new era. Enki outlined their offerings with precision: revolutionary propulsion systems that could drastically reduce travel time between planets, advanced medical technologies capable of curing diseases and extending human lifespans, and sustainable energy solutions that could address the Earth's environmental challenges. Each point was accompanied by detailed projections and models, showcasing the transformative potential of these technologies.

As Enki spoke, the room remained silent, every delegate and expert hanging on his every word. The magnitude of the offer was clear to all present. These advancements were not merely incremental improvements but represented leaps that could change the course of human history. The promise of sustainable energy solutions alone could mitigate climate change, while the medical technologies could revolutionize healthcare globally. The propulsion systems promised to make interstellar travel a reality, aligning perfectly with Musk's vision of a multi-planetary human civilization.

The initial response from the human delegates was one of cautious optimism. They recognized the potential benefits but were also aware of the complexities involved in such a significant exchange. Questions about the logistics, environmental impact, and equitable distribution of these new technologies were raised. The discussion was rigorous, with each point debated thoroughly to ensure that the agreements would be sustainable and beneficial for all parties involved.

The holographic images of Earth, Nibiru, Mars, and the Moon served as constant reminders of the broader context of these negotiations. They highlighted the interconnectedness of the planets and the potential for a collaborative future. The dynamic visuals showed potential mining sites, transportation routes, and joint research facilities, painting a vivid picture of the future they were working towards.

Throughout the discussions, Musk remained a central figure, his expertise in technology and space exploration invaluable. He asked incisive questions about the propulsion systems, probing their capabilities and limitations. His interest in the technological advancements was evident, and he pushed for clarity on how these technologies could be integrated with current human systems. Musk's visionary thinking and practical knowledge helped bridge the gap between the ambitious goals and the technical realities.

As the negotiations continued, it became clear that both sides were committed to finding common ground. The atmosphere in the hall shifted from one of cautious anticipation to a more collaborative and optimistic tone. The mutual respect between the human delegates and the Anunnaki representatives grew, and the discussions became more fluid and productive.

The agreement that began to take shape was one of mutual benefit and shared vision. The world watched as the details were hammered out, the stakes high and the potential for a new era of cooperation within reach. The presence of the Anunnaki, with their advanced knowledge and technology, offered humanity a chance to leap forward in ways that had once seemed like science fiction. The negotiations were the first step in what promised to be a transformative partnership, one that could unlock new potentials for both civilizations and pave the way for a future defined by collaboration and innovation.

Elon Musk was eager to learn about their propulsion technology, which could revolutionize space travel. His eyes sparkled with a blend of excitement and determination, the weight of the moment clear on his face. With an air of excitement tempered by professionalism, he stood before the assembly, ready to present humanity's achievements in space exploration. His presentation was meticulously prepared, filled with data, images, and animations that showcased the milestones achieved by SpaceX and other space agencies.

Musk began by outlining the current state of space travel, highlighting significant accomplishments such as reusable rockets, the successful deployment of the Starlink satellite network, and the ongoing efforts to send crewed missions to Mars. He spoke passionately about humanity's innate desire to explore, to push boundaries, and to secure a future among the stars. His vision for a multi-planetary species was clear, and he emphasized that advanced propulsion technology from the Anunnaki could be the key to making this vision a reality.

He outlined the potential benefits of Anunnaki technology with precision. Advanced propulsion systems, Musk explained, could drastically reduce travel time between planets, making space travel more practical and sustainable. He illustrated how current missions to Mars, which take months, could be shortened to mere weeks, significantly reducing the physical and psychological strain on astronauts. This would not only facilitate quicker missions but also enable more frequent trips, accelerating the process of colonization and exploration.

Musk emphasized the mutual benefits of such an exchange. By integrating Anunnaki propulsion technology, humanity could explore beyond the solar system, potentially reaching exoplanets and other star systems within a human lifetime. He highlighted how this technology could also reduce the costs associated with space travel, making it more accessible and opening up new economic opportunities. The reduction in travel time would enhance safety, lowering the risks associated with prolonged space missions.

As Musk spoke, the room was filled with an air of anticipation. Delegates, scientists, and engineers leaned forward, captivated by the possibilities he described. The combination of human ingenuity and Anunnaki technology seemed to hold limitless potential. Enki, seated across from Musk, listened intently, his expression one of thoughtful consideration.

Enki responded positively, acknowledging the impressive strides humans had made in space exploration. He expressed admiration for the innovative approaches taken by Musk and his team, recognizing the shared spirit of discovery and advancement. Enki then detailed the capabilities of Anunnaki propulsion technology, providing a glimpse into a future that seemed almost fantastical.

He described energy-efficient drives that utilized advanced plasma and fusion technologies, capable of achieving speeds that reduced travel time to Mars from months to mere weeks. These drives operated on principles that combined gravitational manipulation with advanced ion thrusters, allowing for rapid acceleration and deceleration. Enki explained that the potential applications of this technology were vast, including faster interstellar travel, reduced operational costs, and enhanced safety protocols.

The room buzzed with excitement as scientists and engineers envisioned the possibilities. Discussions broke out in hushed tones, as experts began to sketch out potential designs and applications on their tablets and notebooks. The excitement was palpable, a shared sense of wonder at the new horizons that were being opened.

However, amidst the enthusiasm, Lord Enlil, focused on strategic and security concerns, raised important questions about the potential misuse of such powerful technology. He spoke with a measured tone, emphasizing the need for caution and responsibility. Enlil's concerns were not unfounded; the introduction of such advanced technology required careful oversight to prevent its misuse.

It was agreed that strict protocols and shared oversight would be necessary to ensure that these advancements were used responsibly and for the benefit of all humanity. The establishment of joint regulatory bodies and monitoring systems was proposed, involving both human and Anunnaki representatives. This collaborative approach aimed to create a framework that balanced innovation with ethical considerations.

This cautious approach reassured many delegates, who were concerned about the ethical implications of such a technological leap. The idea of shared oversight and international cooperation resonated well, reflecting a commitment to transparency and mutual accountability. The agreement to proceed with caution and respect for the profound impact of these advancements set a positive tone for the negotiations.

As the discussions continued, the sense of optimism and collaboration grew stronger. The prospect of leveraging Anunnaki technology to enhance human space exploration was no longer a distant dream but a tangible goal within reach. The partnership between humanity and the Anunnaki promised to usher in a new era of discovery and progress, grounded in shared values and a commitment to the responsible use of technology.

The discussion then shifted to the terms of the trade. The atmosphere in the grand conference hall grew more intense as the focus turned to the specifics of what each side would offer and receive. The Anunnaki revealed the existence of ancient facilities on Mars and the Moon, remnants of civilizations even older than theirs. These facilities, they explained, could serve as invaluable bases for human exploration and colonization, providing a head start in the quest to become a multi-planetary species.

Enki, ever the meticulous scientist, presented detailed maps and schematics. The holographic projections displayed the locations of these ancient sites, highlighting areas rich in historical artifacts and advanced technology waiting to be rediscovered. The imagery was breathtaking: vast underground complexes on Mars with intact life support systems, and lunar installations equipped with machinery for processing and manufacturing under low-gravity conditions. These facilities held the promise of unlocking new scientific and technological advancements, providing humanity with the resources and infrastructure needed to expand beyond Earth.

In return, the Anunnaki requested access to Earth's gold and water, essential resources for their home planet's survival and technological maintenance. The logistics of extraction were complex but feasible. Detailed plans were drafted, outlining sustainable and environmentally friendly methods for resource extraction. Engineers and environmental scientists collaborated to ensure that the processes would have minimal impact on Earth's ecosystems. Techniques such as deep-sea mining for gold and the use of advanced filtration systems for water extraction were proposed, designed to preserve natural habitats and maintain ecological balance.

Both parties agreed on the importance of preserving the planet while meeting the needs of Nibiru. This shared commitment to environmental stewardship was a cornerstone of the negotiations, reflecting a mutual respect for the delicate balance of life. The Anunnaki's technological expertise in resource extraction, coupled with human ingenuity in environmental conservation, promised to create a sustainable model for resource exchange.

Negotiations on the quantity and timelines for resource transfer were intense but ultimately fruitful. Representatives from both sides worked tirelessly, their discussions filled with technical details and strategic considerations. The debates were rigorous, with each party advocating for terms that would ensure fairness and sustainability. In the end, it was decided that the Anunnaki would assist in establishing efficient extraction and transport systems. Their advanced technology would be leveraged to streamline the process, making it both cost-effective and environmentally sound.

This collaborative approach promised to make the exchange mutually beneficial and sustainable in the long term. The agreement included provisions for continuous monitoring and periodic reviews to assess the impact of the extraction processes and make necessary adjustments. Both sides committed to transparency and open communication, ensuring that the partnership remained equitable and focused on the common good.

Enki's presentation of the ancient facilities had sparked a wave of excitement among the human delegates. Scientists and archaeologists were eager to explore these sites, their minds racing with the possibilities of what they might find. The prospect of uncovering advanced technology from civilizations predating even the Anunnaki was tantalizing, promising to shed light on the early history of the solar system and provide insights that could drive future innovations.

On the other side, the Anunnaki viewed the partnership as a vital step towards ensuring the survival and prosperity of their species. Access to Earth's gold and water would stabilize their home planet's environment and support their technological infrastructure. The advanced extraction methods developed through this collaboration would set a new standard for resource management, benefiting both Earth and Nibiru.

As the negotiations concluded, the room buzzed with a sense of accomplishment and optimism. The agreement represented a significant milestone in human-Anunnaki relations, laying the groundwork for a partnership based on mutual respect and shared goals. The successful conclusion of these discussions was a testament to the power of cooperation and the potential for interstellar collaboration to address common challenges.

The world watched as the details of the agreement were announced, filled with a renewed sense of hope and excitement for the future. The promise of technological advancements, combined with a commitment to environmental sustainability, captured the imagination of people everywhere. This partnership, forged in the spirit of exploration and progress, held the promise of transforming humanity's place in the universe and building a future defined by knowledge, cooperation, and shared purpose.

The negotiations also covered other areas of potential collaboration, opening doors to numerous opportunities for both civilizations to benefit and grow. The Anunnaki offered groundbreaking advancements in medical technology, presenting treatments for diseases that had long plagued humanity. They shared detailed knowledge of regenerative medicine, capable of repairing and even replacing damaged tissues and organs with remarkable precision and efficiency. Their genetic engineering techniques promised to eradicate hereditary diseases and enhance human resilience to various health conditions. Moreover, they introduced advanced prosthetics, which integrated seamlessly with the human nervous system, offering mobility and functionality that far surpassed current technologies. These medical innovations held the promise of revolutionizing healthcare and significantly extending human lifespans, bringing hope to millions suffering from chronic illnesses and disabilities.

In return, humans offered their expertise in various fields, including digital technology and artificial intelligence, which intrigued the Anunnaki. Human advancements in AI, machine learning, and data analytics presented new avenues for the Anunnaki to enhance their own systems. The synergy between Anunnaki biological technology and human digital innovation promised to create hybrid solutions that were more powerful and efficient than either could achieve alone. Collaborative projects were proposed to integrate human AI with Anunnaki medical systems, optimizing diagnostics and treatment plans with unprecedented accuracy and speed.

Furthermore, the Anunnaki proposed joint scientific ventures to explore the ancient facilities on Mars and the Moon. These expeditions would be truly collaborative, combining human curiosity, adaptability, and innovative thinking with Anunnaki experience, wisdom, and advanced technology. The primary goal of these missions was to uncover the secrets of ancient civilizations, whose technological prowess might hold solutions to modern challenges. Detailed plans were made to assemble mixed teams of scientists, archaeologists, engineers, and historians from both civilizations. These teams would work together to excavate, study, and reverse-engineer the ancient technologies, aiming to apply their wisdom to contemporary issues such as sustainable energy, architecture, and even socio-political organization.

Cultural exchange programs were also discussed, with the goal of fostering mutual understanding and respect. The Anunnaki expressed a deep interest in Earth's diverse cultures, arts, and philosophies. They were fascinated by the vast array of human artistic expressions, from music and literature to visual arts and dance, each reflecting different aspects of the human experience. In return, they offered to share their own rich heritage, which encompassed millennia of history, art, literature, and philosophical thought. The Anunnaki cultural heritage included intricate oral traditions, sophisticated musical compositions, and profound philosophical texts that explored the nature of existence, ethics, and the cosmos.

This cultural exchange promised to enrich both civilizations, promoting peace and cooperation through a deeper understanding of each other's values and traditions. Programs were envisioned that would include cultural festivals, art exhibitions, academic exchanges, and joint creative projects. These initiatives aimed to break down barriers and build bridges of empathy and respect. Schools and universities on Earth and Nibiru would host exchange students and scholars, fostering a new generation of leaders who appreciated the strengths and beauty of both cultures.

The integration of Anunnaki and human knowledge extended beyond technology and culture to encompass environmental stewardship. The Anunnaki shared advanced techniques for environmental management, including methods to restore ecosystems and mitigate climate change. Joint projects were proposed to apply these techniques to rehabilitate damaged areas on Earth, ensuring sustainable development and biodiversity conservation.

As the negotiations drew to a close, the agreements reached were comprehensive and forward-thinking, setting the stage for an era of unprecedented collaboration and progress. The world watched with hopeful anticipation as leaders from both civilizations signed the accords, symbolizing the beginning of a new chapter in interstellar relations. The exchange of knowledge, resources, and culture promised to elevate both humanity and the Anunnaki, forging a partnership that would navigate the challenges of the future with wisdom and unity.

After days of intense negotiations, a historic agreement was reached. The culmination of discussions, debates, and mutual compromises resulted in a landmark accord that symbolized a new dawn in interstellar relations. The world watched with bated breath as representatives from both sides gathered in a grand ceremony to sign the accords, marking the beginning of a new era of cooperation between humans and the Anunnaki. The signing ceremony, held in a magnificent hall adorned with symbols of both civilizations, was broadcast live across the globe, with billions tuning in to witness the momentous occasion.

The agreement was comprehensive, covering every aspect necessary to ensure a fruitful partnership. It detailed the terms of resource exchange, where Earth would provide the Anunnaki with gold and water essential for their survival. In return, the Anunnaki committed to sharing their advanced technologies, including propulsion systems, medical breakthroughs, and sustainable energy solutions. The accord also outlined joint scientific endeavors, particularly the exploration of ancient facilities on Mars and the Moon. These expeditions promised to unveil secrets of civilizations even older than the Anunnaki, potentially offering insights that could revolutionize modern science and technology.

Moreover, the agreement emphasized cultural exchanges, recognizing the profound importance of mutual understanding and respect. Programs were established to facilitate the sharing of art, music, literature, and philosophy, enriching both cultures and fostering a sense of global unity. Educational institutions prepared to welcome Anunnaki scholars, while human students and researchers were eager to learn from their extraterrestrial counterparts.

The announcement of the agreement was met with global celebration. News outlets from every corner of the world broadcasted the details, highlighting the immense potential benefits for all of humanity. Headlines proclaimed the dawn of a new era, and special segments delved into the specifics of the technologies and collaborations that were now within reach. Social media platforms buzzed with excitement, as people expressed their hopes and dreams for the future. The promise of advanced technology, medical breakthroughs, and the possibility of exploring ancient extraterrestrial ruins captured the imagination of billions. Public response was overwhelmingly positive, with communities and individuals alike embracing the potential for progress and unity.

As the Anunnaki prepared to return to their home planet with the first shipments of gold and water, they left behind teams of scientists and engineers to continue the collaborative projects. These mixed teams symbolized the commitment to ongoing partnership and mutual growth. The exchange of knowledge and resources had begun in earnest, setting humanity on a path towards unprecedented progress and exploration. Laboratories and research centers buzzed with activity, as human and Anunnaki experts worked side by side, pushing the boundaries of what was possible.

The arrival of the Anunnaki had marked the beginning of a new era, and the successful negotiations solidified this partnership. Guided by the hope that understanding and unity could light the way forward, humans and Anunnaki embarked on a shared journey to unlock the mysteries of the universe and build a future defined by knowledge, cooperation, and shared purpose. The spirit of collaboration was palpable, inspiring new initiatives and projects that aimed to address global challenges, from environmental sustainability to space colonization.

The world stood united, ready to embrace the limitless possibilities that lay ahead. Educational institutions adapted their curricula to include new fields of study based on Anunnaki knowledge, while cultural festivals celebrated the fusion of human and Anunnaki traditions. Economies began to adapt to the influx of new technologies, creating jobs and industries that had previously been the stuff of science fiction.

As the days turned into months, the fruits of the partnership began to manifest. Medical facilities saw the introduction of advanced Anunnaki treatments, significantly improving health outcomes and extending lifespans. Energy grids started integrating sustainable solutions provided by the Anunnaki, reducing reliance on fossil fuels and mitigating climate change. Space missions equipped with new propulsion technologies made rapid progress, bringing the dream of Mars colonization closer to reality.

In communities worldwide, the sense of hope and excitement persisted. Children dreamed of becoming astronauts, scientists, and ambassadors in this new interstellar age. Artists and creators found inspiration in the fusion of human and Anunnaki cultures, producing works that reflected the shared journey of both civilizations.

CHAPTER 6: SECRETS OF THE MOON

Enki led Elon Musk and a select team of scientists, engineers, and archaeologists on a journey to the Moon, a mission that promised to unveil secrets that had eluded humanity for centuries. The team, handpicked for their expertise and innovative thinking, represented the best of human achievement. Each member brought a unique set of skills and a deep sense of curiosity, united by the common goal of unlocking the mysteries that lay hidden beneath the Moon's surface. Their backgrounds varied widely, from astrophysics and robotics to ancient history and linguistics, creating a multidisciplinary approach that was critical for the success of the mission.

They boarded a specially designed spacecraft, a marvel of engineering that combined the ingenuity of human technology with the advanced capabilities of the Anunnaki. The sleek, aerodynamic exterior of the craft was built for both speed and stability, while the interior was a harmonious blend of functionality and futuristic design. Advanced navigation systems, enhanced life support mechanisms, and sophisticated communication arrays were seamlessly integrated into the spacecraft, ensuring that the team could operate efficiently and stay connected with Earth and the Anunnaki command centers.

As they settled into their seats, the air was filled with a mix of awe and anticipation. The realization that they were about to embark on a historic journey to uncover secrets buried for millennia weighed heavily on their minds. The spacecraft's engines roared to life, and with a smooth lift-off, they began their ascent, leaving Earth behind. The journey through space was punctuated by discussions and briefings, as Enki shared insights about what they might expect and prepared them for the discoveries ahead.

As the spacecraft approached the Moon, the familiar sight of its cratered surface filled the windows. The stark, desolate beauty of the lunar landscape was mesmerizing, each crater and ridge telling a story of cosmic impacts and geological history. However, Enki's calm demeanor suggested that what they were about to discover went far beyond the surface. His presence was reassuring, a steady anchor amidst the team's growing excitement and curiosity.

The landing site was a relatively flat area near the Moon's equator, strategically chosen for its proximity to an entrance to the hollow interior that the Anunnaki had repurposed millennia ago. The site appeared unremarkable at first glance, blending seamlessly with the surrounding lunar terrain. Yet, it held the promise of unparalleled discoveries. The spacecraft touched down with a gentle thud, the landing precision a testament to the advanced technology at their disposal.

The team disembarked, their boots kicking up the fine lunar dust that settled slowly back to the ground in the Moon's low gravity. The experience of walking on the lunar surface was surreal, each step a reminder of the extraordinary nature of their mission. The Anunnaki, with their knowledge and experience, led them to a seemingly nondescript area. Enki, with a confident and purposeful stride, approached a specific spot and activated a concealed mechanism with a series of precise hand movements.

The ground rumbled softly, a subtle vibration that could be felt through their feet. Slowly, a large section of the lunar surface began to slide open, revealing a sleek, metallic passageway leading deep into the Moon's interior. The passageway, illuminated by a soft, ambient light, beckoned them forward, promising to unveil the secrets of an ancient civilization that had once thrived within the Moon. The team, filled with a sense of wonder and anticipation, prepared to step into the unknown, ready to uncover the mysteries that had eluded humanity for so long.

The team descended into the passageway, the walls glowing with a soft, ambient light that seemed to emanate from within the metal itself. This light was unlike any artificial illumination they had encountered before, its source invisible yet pervasive, bathing the corridor in a gentle, ethereal glow. The material of the walls felt almost alive, pulsating subtly as if in response to their presence, hinting at the advanced technology that powered this hidden interior.

As they moved deeper, the tunnel widened into a vast, cavernous space, revealing the hollow nature of the Moon. The sheer scale of the interior was staggering, a hidden world within the familiar celestial body. Towering structures reached upwards, their tops disappearing into the heights of the cavern. Intricate machinery, both ancient and highly sophisticated, stretched out as far as the eye could see, a labyrinth of technological marvels. The enormity of the space suggested a purpose far beyond mere habitation, hinting at a complex and multifaceted operation.

Enki, leading the way with an air of calm authority, began to explain the origins and purpose of this extraordinary place. He revealed that the Moon was a hollow construct, possibly placed by an ancient race over a billion years ago. This revelation left the team speechless. The Moon, a constant presence in the night sky, was not a natural satellite but an artifact of advanced engineering. The notion that it had been deliberately positioned and utilized by an ancient civilization was almost too incredible to comprehend.

The Anunnaki had discovered this hollow Moon during their own explorations and had repurposed it to process gold, exploiting the low gravity for easier transport to their home planet. Enki's explanation was accompanied by gestural illustrations, his hands tracing the history and functions of the various structures they encountered. The team absorbed this information in a state of awe, realizing that they were standing inside a construct that had served as both a hub of activity and a monument to ancient ingenuity.

They walked through corridors lined with massive, dormant machines that hummed with latent energy. The air was filled with a subtle vibration, the pulse of technologies that had been dormant for millennia but still held power. These machines, towering and intricate, seemed almost to watch them, silent guardians of secrets long hidden. Enki pointed out areas where the Anunnaki had installed their own technology, blending seamlessly with the original designs. These additions, though sophisticated, were respectful of the ancient structure, enhancing its functionality without compromising its integrity.

The Anunnaki had used these facilities to refine and transport gold, turning the Moon into a critical hub for their operations. Enki's descriptions painted a picture of a bustling center of activity, where raw materials were processed and dispatched with efficiency and precision. The fusion of ancient and Anunnaki technology was a testament to their adaptability and resourcefulness. Machines of varying sizes and purposes stood silent now, their forms both alien and oddly familiar, a bridge between two eras of technological mastery.

The team moved through expansive halls and narrow passageways, each new area revealing more about the scope and sophistication of the operation. Storage areas with vast, empty containers hinted at the scale of the gold processing that had taken place here. Control rooms with complex interfaces suggested advanced computational abilities, while transport docks indicated a once-active logistics network.

Everywhere they looked, the seamless integration of Anunnaki technology with the ancient constructs spoke of a deep respect for the original builders. It was clear that the Anunnaki had not merely occupied this space but had become stewards of its legacy, maintaining its functions while adding their own advanced systems to enhance its capabilities.

The enormity of their discoveries began to sink in, a mix of exhilaration and humility. They were standing within a relic of immense historical and technological significance, a testament to the boundless possibilities of intelligent life in the universe. The knowledge that the Moon was not a natural satellite but an engineered artifact opened up endless questions about its creators and their intentions.

The discovery of such ancient technology left humanity in awe. The sense of wonder and astonishment was palpable as the team explored the vast interior, their instruments capturing data and images at every step. They moved methodically through the colossal space, their sophisticated equipment documenting every detail with precision. The atmosphere was charged with excitement and reverence, a mix of scientific curiosity and the profound realization that they were treading on the legacy of an ancient, advanced civilization.

They found enormous halls filled with rows of intricate devices, whose purposes were not immediately clear. These devices, crafted with a complexity and finesse that defied current human understanding, stood as silent sentinels of a bygone era. Some appeared to be reactors of some sort, possibly powering the entire structure with an efficiency that modern scientists could only dream of. The reactors hummed with a faint, steady energy, their inner workings a mystery that beckoned to be solved. Others resembled communication arrays or computational nodes, intricate networks of conduits and interfaces that suggested a highly sophisticated means of data processing and transmission.

Elon Musk was particularly fascinated by the propulsion systems integrated into the Moon's infrastructure. His eyes lit up with a blend of excitement and determination as Enki demonstrated how these systems had once enabled the Moon to move through space. The propulsion mechanisms, embedded seamlessly into the structure, were a marvel of engineering. Enki explained how they could manipulate gravitational fields and utilize advanced energy sources to propel the Moon across vast distances. This revelation suggested that the Moon could have been repositioned by its creators, potentially serving as a mobile base or a strategic station.

Musk's mind raced with possibilities, envisioning the applications of such technology for human space travel and colonization efforts. He saw potential beyond mere propulsion, these systems could revolutionize the way humans approached interstellar travel, making the dream of exploring distant planets and even other star systems a tangible reality. The integration of such advanced propulsion technology could drastically reduce travel times, enhance safety, and open new frontiers for human settlement and resource acquisition.

The archaeologists on the team were equally captivated by what they found. They discovered inscriptions and artifacts that hinted at the culture and knowledge of the ancient race that had constructed the Moon. These artifacts, incredibly well-preserved in the vacuum of the Moon's interior, offered a direct link to a civilization that had mastered technologies far beyond human comprehension. The objects ranged from everyday tools to ceremonial items, each meticulously crafted and rich with symbolic meaning.

The symbols and writings bore no resemblance to any known languages, presenting a tantalizing mystery for linguists and historians to unravel. The inscriptions, etched into the walls and various artifacts, were composed of intricate patterns and glyphs that suggested a complex system of communication. The archaeologists meticulously documented these symbols, aware that deciphering them could unlock invaluable insights into the thought processes, beliefs, and technological advancements of the Moon's creators.

As they continued their exploration, the team was struck by the seamless integration of form and function in the artifacts they discovered. Every object, no matter how utilitarian, was also a work of art, reflecting a culture that valued both efficiency and aesthetic beauty. The artifacts told a story of a civilization that had achieved a high level of technological and cultural sophistication, yet had vanished from history, leaving behind only these silent remnants.

The discovery of these ancient technologies and artifacts was more than just a scientific breakthrough, it was a profound reminder of humanity's place in the universe. It underscored the vastness of cosmic history and the potential for other intelligent civilizations that might have risen and fallen long before humans emerged. This revelation inspired a deep sense of humility and a renewed commitment to exploration and discovery.

The team's instruments continued to capture and transmit data, each new piece of information adding to the growing body of knowledge about this enigmatic place. The scientists, engineers, and archaeologists knew that their findings would have far-reaching implications, not only for their own fields but for humanity as a whole. The ancient technologies they had uncovered held the promise of revolutionizing modern science and engineering, while the cultural artifacts provided a unique window into the minds of an ancient, advanced race.

In the cavernous halls of the Moon, surrounded by the remnants of a civilization long gone, the team felt a deep connection to the broader tapestry of the cosmos. They were not just explorers but inheritors of a legacy that spanned the millennia. Their mission had only just begun, but already it had reshaped their understanding of the universe and their place within it. The secrets of the Moon, once hidden and elusive, were now within reach, offering a wealth of knowledge and inspiration for generations to come.

The enormity of their discoveries led the team to reflect deeply on how little humanity truly understood about its place in the universe. Standing within the vast, hollow interior of the Moon, surrounded by technology and artifacts from an ancient civilization, they were struck by a profound sense of humility. The existence of such advanced ancient technology was a humbling reminder of the vastness of cosmic history, a history that extended far beyond the relatively brief span of human existence. It was a powerful realization that the universe was far older and more complex than they had ever imagined, and that humanity was but a small part of a much larger tapestry.

This realization challenged their perceptions and encouraged a deeper curiosity about the origins of intelligent life and the potential for other civilizations beyond their own. The knowledge that the Moon was an engineered construct, placed in orbit by a race that had achieved unimaginable technological feats, opened up new avenues of thought and inquiry. The team began to question everything they knew about the development of intelligent life, the evolution of technology, and the likelihood of other advanced civilizations existing elsewhere in the universe.

Enki's revelations about the Moon's history underscored the interconnectedness of all life in the cosmos. He spoke of the Anunnaki's own journey of discovery, recounting their encounters with other ancient races and the wealth of knowledge they had gained along the way. Enki's stories painted a picture of a universe teeming with life, each civilization contributing to a collective understanding of existence. The story of the Moon, with its ancient origins and repurposed functionality, was but one chapter in a much larger narrative, one that humanity was now a part of.

The team felt a profound sense of responsibility as they absorbed the implications of their discoveries. The knowledge they were gaining had the potential to transform human civilization in ways they could scarcely imagine, but it also came with the duty to use it wisely. The advanced technologies they were uncovering held the promise of revolutionizing fields such as energy, transportation, medicine, and communication. However, the ethical considerations of such powerful advancements weighed heavily on their minds.

They discussed the implications of their findings at length, recognizing that with great power came great responsibility. The potential for new technologies was immense, but so too were the risks. The team debated how best to share this knowledge with the world, considering the potential benefits and the dangers of misuse. They understood that the integration of such advanced technology into human society would need to be handled with care, ensuring that it was used for the betterment of all and not for destructive purposes.

Moreover, they contemplated the broader philosophical and ethical questions raised by their discoveries. What were the responsibilities of a civilization that possessed such advanced knowledge? How should they engage with other potential civilizations in the universe? What lessons could they learn from the ancient race that had created the Moon, and how could they apply those lessons to avoid repeating past mistakes?

As they delved deeper into these questions, the team was united by a common purpose. They were not just explorers and scientists; they were stewards of a legacy that transcended time and space. Their mission was to ensure that the knowledge and technology they uncovered would be used to advance human civilization in a responsible and ethical manner. They envisioned a future where humanity could harness these ancient technologies to solve some of its most pressing problems, from climate change and energy scarcity to disease and poverty.

The weight of their discoveries was balanced by a sense of

hope and possibility. They felt a renewed commitment to the principles of exploration, curiosity, and ethical responsibility. The story of the Moon, with its hidden depths and ancient secrets, had become a part of their own narrative. They were now part of a continuum of discovery that stretched back billions of years and would continue into the future, guided by the lessons of the past and the promise of new horizons.

In this moment of reflection, the team recognized that their journey was not just about uncovering the mysteries of the Moon. It was about understanding their place in the universe and embracing the responsibilities that came with such profound knowledge. The path ahead was filled with challenges and uncertainties, but it was also illuminated by the potential for unprecedented growth and understanding. As they stood in the vast interior of the Moon, the team was united by a shared vision of a future where knowledge, wisdom, and ethical stewardship would guide humanity to new heights.

As their exploration of the Moon's interior continued, the team began to catalog and analyze the technology and artifacts they encountered. Each discovery was meticulously documented, with data being recorded, samples collected, and images captured. Advanced scanners and 3D imaging technology were employed to create detailed models of the machinery and structures they found. Every piece of technology, from the smallest component to the largest reactor, was scrutinized to understand its function and potential applications.

Enki and Musk worked closely, their collaboration embodying the merging of ancient wisdom and modern innovation. Enki provided insights into the principles and history behind the ancient technologies, while Musk offered expertise on how these could be adapted and integrated into contemporary human technological frameworks. Together, they brainstormed ideas and developed preliminary plans to incorporate these advanced systems into existing infrastructures on Earth.

They planned to share their findings with the broader scientific community, ensuring that the benefits of this ancient wisdom would be accessible to all. This transparency was crucial; it not only fostered global collaboration but also ensured that the knowledge would be used ethically and responsibly. Detailed reports, comprehensive datasets, and high-resolution images were prepared for dissemination to research institutions, universities, and think tanks around the world. Conferences and symposiums were planned to present the discoveries, inviting experts from various fields to contribute to the understanding and application of the newfound technologies.

The collaborative spirit between the Anunnaki and humans grew stronger with each passing day. The shared goal of unlocking the Moon's secrets created a bond of mutual respect and admiration. Joint research initiatives were proposed, focusing on reverse-engineering the ancient technologies and understanding the principles behind them. These initiatives aimed to replicate and perhaps even enhance the functionalities of the ancient devices, applying them to solve contemporary challenges such as energy sustainability, medical advancements, and space travel.

Training programs were envisioned to educate a new generation of scientists and engineers, capable of bridging the gap between human and Anunnaki knowledge. These programs would be comprehensive, covering both theoretical and practical aspects of the ancient technologies. Universities and research institutions were expected to offer specialized courses and degrees, fostering a cadre of experts proficient in this hybrid field. Exchange programs were also discussed, allowing students and researchers to work directly with Anunnaki scientists, gaining firsthand experience and fostering deeper intercultural understanding.

As the mission on the Moon came to a close, the team prepared to return to Earth with their findings. They carried with them not only data and artifacts but also a renewed sense of purpose and a vision for the future. Their time on the Moon had been transformative, expanding their horizons and reinforcing the importance of knowledge and cooperation. The artifacts they brought back were not just relics of the past but keys to a future where advanced technology could enhance human life in ways previously unimaginable.

The successful collaboration on the Moon set a powerful precedent for future endeavors, reinforcing the potential of what humanity and the Anunnaki could achieve together. This mission was a testament to the power of unity and the shared pursuit of knowledge. It demonstrated that when different civilizations come together, they can overcome challenges and achieve extraordinary results. The lessons learned and the relationships forged during this mission would guide future collaborations, inspiring joint projects on Earth and beyond.

The world awaited their return, eager to hear the stories and see the discoveries that would shape the next chapter of human history. News of the mission's success had already begun to spread, creating a buzz of anticipation. People from all walks of life, from schoolchildren to seasoned scientists, were excited to learn about the technologies and artifacts that had been uncovered. The mission's findings promised to spark a wave of innovation and exploration, driving humanity forward into a new era of discovery and progress.

CHAPTER 7: MARS UNVEILED

The journey continued to Mars, where abandoned Anunnaki facilities dotted the landscape like silent sentinels of a bygone era. As the spacecraft descended towards the red planet, Elon Musk and his team eagerly anticipated the next phase of their mission. The sight of Mars, with its dusty plains stretching endlessly and its towering volcanoes piercing the thin atmosphere, was both familiar and thrilling. Each feature of the Martian terrain, from the vast Valles Marineris to the imposing Olympus Mons, seemed to whisper secrets of ancient times.

The ancient structures visible from orbit hinted at a time when Mars had been a thriving hub of activity. These remnants, scattered across the planet's surface, bore testament to the sophisticated civilization that had once flourished there. Enki stood beside Musk in the control room, observing the planet's surface with a mix of pride and nostalgia. His eyes, reflecting the soft glow of the control panels, took in the landscape that had once been the epicenter of Anunnaki innovation.

"This is where it all began for our operations in your solar system," Enki said, his voice filled with nostalgia and a touch of melancholy. The memories of bustling research stations, vibrant communities, and groundbreaking discoveries played out in his mind, contrasting sharply with the desolate silence that now reigned.

Musk nodded, his eyes scanning the landscape with a blend of awe and determination. "It's incredible to think that millions of years ago, this planet was bustling with life and technology. I'm eager to learn how we can use what you left behind to aid our colonization efforts." His voice carried a sense of urgency and excitement, reflecting his vision of a future where Mars could once again support life.

Enki smiled, a gesture that conveyed both warmth and a shared sense of purpose. "We have much to show you. The technology here is old, but still very advanced. It will provide valuable insights and practical tools for your plans." His words were filled with promise, hinting at the vast potential that lay hidden beneath the Martian surface.

As the spacecraft prepared for landing, the team members gathered their equipment, their minds buzzing with anticipation. They knew that the ancient Anunnaki facilities held the key to overcoming many of the challenges they faced in making Mars a new home for humanity. The prospect of exploring these relics, understanding their mechanisms, and adapting them to modern needs was both daunting and exhilarating.

The spacecraft touched down with a gentle thud, its landing struts sinking slightly into the Martian dust. The ramp extended, and Musk, Enki, and the rest of the team disembarked, their boots kicking up small clouds of reddish soil. The air was thin and cold, but the excitement of discovery warmed them.

They stood for a moment, taking in the view of the vast, open landscape, punctuated by the distant silhouettes of the ancient structures. Each member of the team felt the weight of history upon them, aware that they were about to walk in the footsteps of a civilization that had achieved wonders long before humans had even dreamed of reaching the stars.

Enki led the way to the nearest facility, a colossal structure partially buried in the dust. Its walls, though weathered by time, still stood strong, a testament to the durability of Anunnaki engineering. The entrance, marked by intricate carvings and symbols, seemed to invite them into a world of ancient knowledge and advanced technology.

Musk and his team followed Enki, their senses heightened by the significance of the moment. The interior of the facility, though dormant, exuded a sense of purpose and potential. The team could almost hear the echoes of past activities, the hum of machines, and the voices of the Anunnaki who had once called this place home.

As they ventured further into the structure, the true scale of the Anunnaki's achievements began to unfold before them. The halls were lined with dormant machinery and advanced equipment, each piece waiting to be reawakened. The team moved with a mix of reverence and eagerness, ready to unlock the secrets that Mars held.

Enki's promise of valuable insights and practical tools resonated deeply with Musk. He envisioned the day when human colonies on Mars would thrive, powered by the technology and knowledge inherited from the Anunnaki. This journey was not just about exploration; it was about forging a new future, one that honored the past while boldly stepping into the unknown.

In the silence of the Martian landscape, the collaboration between humans and Anunnaki took on a profound significance. It was a testament to the enduring spirit of discovery and the boundless possibilities that lay ahead. As they began their work, the team knew that they were not just uncovering the past; they were building the foundations of a new chapter in human history, one that would be written in the dust of Mars.

Once on the surface, the team disembarked and made their way to the nearest Anunnaki facility. The sight that greeted them was awe-inspiring: the structure was immense, towering above the barren landscape, a testament to the engineering prowess of its creators. The walls, crafted from a durable, metallic alloy, had withstood the test of time, bearing the scars of countless sandstorms and meteorite impacts yet remaining fundamentally intact. Despite the wear and tear, the integrity of the design was evident, showcasing the advanced engineering capabilities of the Anunnaki. The architecture combined functionality with an almost artistic elegance, each line and curve serving a purpose while also contributing to an overall aesthetic that spoke of a deep understanding of both form and function.

As they entered the facility, the transition from the harsh exterior to the sheltered interior was palpable. The temperature dropped, and the howling winds of Mars were left behind, replaced by a hushed silence. Enki, guiding the team with a steady hand, pointed out various features that highlighted the sophistication of Anunnaki technology. "These halls were once filled with researchers and engineers," he began, his voice echoing slightly in the expansive corridor. "We developed many technologies here that we later used on other planets."

The team followed closely, their eyes taking in the vastness of the space. The hallways were lined with intricate patterns and symbols, likely serving both decorative and informational purposes. Illuminated panels along the walls flickered to life as they passed, casting a soft, ambient glow that revealed more of the facility's inner workings. Musk ran his hand along the smooth, metallic wall, feeling the cool surface beneath his fingertips. "The craftsmanship is extraordinary," he remarked, marveling at the seamless joins and the lack of any visible fasteners. "What were these facilities primarily used for?"

Enki led him to a central chamber filled with dormant machinery. The room was vast, with ceilings that seemed to stretch up into the darkness. In the center stood massive, complex machines, their purpose not immediately clear but their importance undeniable. "This was a research and development center," Enki explained, his voice filled with pride and a touch of nostalgia. "We focused on creating sustainable habitats, advanced propulsion systems, and energy-efficient technologies. Many of these innovations can be adapted for your Mars colonization plans."

The central chamber was a treasure trove of technological marvels. Workstations lined the walls, each equipped with advanced interfaces and tools that, even in their dormant state, exuded a sense of sophistication. Holographic displays, now inactive, hinted at the level of data processing and visualization that took place here. Enki walked over to one of the large machines and activated a control panel. Lights flickered on, and the machine hummed to life, its purpose becoming clearer as various parts moved and adjusted. "This device," Enki pointed out, "was used to simulate environmental conditions and test the sustainability of our habitat designs under different scenarios."

Musk and his team moved closer, examining the machinery with keen interest. The potential applications of such a device for their own projects were immediately apparent. They could use it to model and perfect the living conditions for human settlers on Mars, ensuring that habitats would be both safe and comfortable.

The room also contained propulsion systems that Enki highlighted. "These propulsion units were among the first of their kind," he said. "They harness both solar and geothermal energy, making them incredibly efficient. They could power your transport vehicles and even contribute to the overall energy grid of a Martian colony."

Musk's eyes lit up with excitement as he envisioned the possibilities. "Integrating this technology could drastically reduce our energy dependency and increase the sustainability of our operations," he mused. The Anunnaki's innovations in propulsion could revolutionize their approach to moving people and resources across the Martian landscape.

As the team continued their tour of the facility, they discovered numerous other technological wonders. There were automated manufacturing units capable of producing complex components with minimal human intervention, energy storage systems that could hold vast amounts of power with negligible loss, and even bio-engineering labs where sustainable food sources had been developed.

Each discovery reinforced the team's understanding of just how advanced the Anunnaki civilization had been and how much humanity could learn from them. The facility was not just a relic of the past but a blueprint for the future, offering solutions to many of the challenges faced in making Mars a viable home for humans.

The enormity of what they had uncovered began to sink in, filling them with a profound sense of purpose. The collaboration between Musk and Enki, between humans and Anunnaki, was laying the foundation for a new era of exploration and innovation. The ancient technologies and wisdom of the Anunnaki, combined with human ingenuity and determination, promised to unlock the potential of Mars and transform it into a thriving hub of human activity.

The team moved deeper into the facility, their anticipation growing with each step as they encountered rooms filled with a plethora of equipment and data storage devices. The walls of these rooms were lined with advanced machinery and consoles, many of which still hummed softly with latent energy. Each device, though covered in a thin layer of Martian dust, retained a sense of purpose and sophistication. It was clear that these rooms had been the nerve centers of the facility's operations, where cutting-edge research and development had taken place.

Enki approached one of the larger consoles and began to activate it with a series of precise commands. The console responded immediately, its surface lighting up with a soft, blue glow. Holographic displays sprang to life, filling the room with a cascade of floating diagrams, technical specifications, and complex models. The holograms were incredibly detailed, showing every aspect of the projects that had been undertaken here.

Musk watched intently as the displays materialized in mid-air. His eyes darted from one diagram to another, absorbing the wealth of information presented before him. Enki pointed to a set of detailed blueprints and began to explain. "These propulsion systems," he said, his voice steady and clear, "were designed to operate in Mars' unique environment. They harness both solar and geothermal energy, ensuring a constant power supply even during dust storms."

Musk's eyes widened with excitement as he studied the propulsion systems. The diagrams showed advanced energy collectors and converters that could efficiently tap into Mars' natural resources. "This could solve one of our biggest challenges," he said, his voice filled with enthusiasm. "Reliable energy sources are crucial for sustaining life on Mars. Our current systems are vulnerable to the planet's frequent dust storms and limited sunlight."

Enki nodded, his expression reflecting Musk's excitement. "Exactly. These systems are designed to be resilient and efficient, adapting to the fluctuating conditions on Mars. By combining solar and geothermal energy, they provide a stable and continuous power supply, critical for maintaining life support systems, research operations, and habitat functions."

As they continued to explore the holographic displays, Enki pointed out another set of designs. "And there are also designs for modular habitats that can be easily expanded as your colony grows. They are built to withstand the harsh conditions of Mars while providing comfort and safety."

Musk leaned in closer, examining the habitat models with keen interest. The designs were ingenious, featuring modular units that could be assembled and expanded with relative ease. Each module was equipped with life support systems, thermal insulation, and radiation shielding, ensuring that the inhabitants would remain safe and comfortable regardless of the external conditions. "These habitats are perfect for our needs," Musk remarked. "Their modular nature means we can start small and gradually expand as more settlers arrive. Plus, their robustness against Mars' environment is exactly what we need to ensure long-term sustainability."

Enki smiled, pleased with Musk's reaction. "Indeed. The adaptability and resilience of these habitats will be key to establishing a thriving colony. They can be connected to form larger structures, creating a network of interconnected living and working spaces. This flexibility will allow you to scale your operations efficiently as the colony grows."

The room buzzed with a sense of discovery and potential as the team continued to explore the holographic displays. They saw blueprints for advanced agricultural systems, capable of growing food in Martian soil using minimal water and energy. There were also designs for medical facilities, equipped with cutting-edge technology to ensure the health and well-being of the colonists.

Every aspect of the Anunnaki technology was meticulously detailed, offering solutions to the myriad challenges of living on Mars. The team members exchanged ideas and took copious notes, their minds racing with the possibilities that these ancient innovations presented. It was clear that the knowledge contained within this facility could accelerate humanity's plans for Mars colonization by decades.

The deeper they delved into the data, the more they realized the extent of what was possible. Enki's guidance was invaluable, his explanations providing context and understanding that transformed the ancient designs into actionable plans. The collaboration between the Anunnaki wisdom and human ingenuity was yielding remarkable results, creating a blueprint for a sustainable and prosperous Martian colony.

As the session concluded, the team felt a renewed sense of

purpose and excitement. They had unlocked a treasure trove of knowledge that would not only aid in the colonization of Mars but also push the boundaries of human technology and resilience. The vision of a thriving human settlement on the red planet was becoming clearer and more attainable, driven by the profound discoveries made within the ancient Anunnaki facility.

As the days went by, Musk and the Anunnaki worked closely to integrate the ancient technologies into modern plans for Mars colonization. Their collaboration was marked by a constant buzz of activity, with the team members immersing themselves in the wealth of knowledge available to them. They held frequent discussions, brainstorming sessions, and collaborative workshops, each one more productive than the last. The blend of ancient wisdom and cutting-edge innovation created a dynamic environment where creativity and practicality went hand in hand.

The exchange of ideas was seamless, with both sides bringing unique perspectives to the table. The Anunnaki shared their extensive experience with sustainable living and advanced engineering, while Musk's team contributed their modern scientific understanding and innovative problem-solving skills. The synergy between the two groups was palpable, leading to groundbreaking insights and solutions that neither could have achieved alone.

One evening, as they reviewed plans in the central chamber, the atmosphere was filled with a quiet intensity. Holographic displays illuminated the room, casting a futuristic glow on the faces of the team members as they poured over the intricate designs. Musk turned to Enki, his expression one of deep appreciation. "Your knowledge has been invaluable," he said, his voice reflecting genuine admiration. "We're not just learning about your technology; we're also understanding how you approached problem-solving."

Enki smiled, a warm, thoughtful expression that conveyed both humility and respect. "It's a mutual exchange, Elon. Your team's creativity and determination are inspiring. Together, we can create a thriving colony on Mars, building on the foundations we left behind." His words were filled with a sense of shared purpose and optimism, highlighting the strength of their partnership.

They continued to refine the plans, incorporating Anunnaki advancements in habitat construction, resource management, and transportation. The collaborative effort resulted in innovative designs that were both resilient and adaptable. The habitats were planned with modular components, allowing them to be expanded as the colony grew. These structures were designed to withstand the harsh Martian environment, providing safe and comfortable living spaces for the settlers.

In terms of resource management, the Anunnaki's techniques for harnessing solar and geothermal energy were seamlessly integrated into the colony's infrastructure. This ensured a steady and reliable power supply, crucial for sustaining life on Mars. The advanced agricultural systems designed by the Anunnaki were also adapted, promising to provide the colony with a sustainable source of food using minimal water and energy.

Transportation was another critical aspect they addressed. The Anunnaki's propulsion systems, capable of operating efficiently in Mars' unique environment, were incorporated into the designs for transport vehicles and cargo systems. This ensured that the colony would have the mobility and logistical support needed to explore and develop the planet further.

The goal was to create a sustainable, self-sufficient colony that could grow and adapt over time. Every aspect of the plan was designed with flexibility in mind, allowing the colony to evolve in response to new challenges and opportunities. The collaborative effort between Musk and the Anunnaki was laying the groundwork for a future where humanity could thrive on Mars, not just survive.

As they worked late into the nights, refining and perfecting the plans, a strong sense of camaraderie developed among the team members. They were united by a shared vision and driven by the excitement of pioneering a new chapter in human history. The blend of ancient knowledge and modern ingenuity was creating something truly extraordinary, a blueprint for a Martian colony that embodied the best of both civilizations.

This partnership, born out of mutual respect and a common goal, was setting a powerful precedent for future collaborations. It demonstrated the immense potential that could be unlocked when different cultures and knowledge systems came together. The plans for Mars colonization were more than just technical blueprints; they were a testament to the power of unity and the endless possibilities that lay ahead.

The days of intense collaboration were filled with breakthroughs and discoveries, each one bringing them closer to their goal. The successful integration of Anunnaki technology into human plans for Mars was not just a technological achievement; it was a symbol of hope and progress. It showed that humanity was capable of reaching new heights through cooperation and shared vision.

As the team continued their work, the excitement and anticipation for the future grew. The vision of a thriving, self-sufficient colony on Mars was becoming a reality, driven by the combined efforts of Musk, the Anunnaki, and their dedicated teams. The foundation they were building promised to support a new era of exploration and discovery, one that would expand the horizons of human potential and transform our understanding of the universe.

As the mission on Mars drew to a close, the team prepared to return to Earth with their newfound knowledge. The atmosphere was charged with a mix of triumph and anticipation, knowing they had uncovered secrets that could change the trajectory of human space exploration forever. The collaboration between Musk and the Anunnaki had laid the groundwork for an ambitious colonization project, one that promised to transform the way humanity approached space travel and settlement.

Before departing, Musk and Enki stood on a ridge overlooking the expansive Martian landscape, a breathtaking vista of rust-colored plains, towering mountains, and vast canyons bathed in the soft glow of the setting sun. The sight was both humbling and inspiring, a stark reminder of the challenges that lay ahead and the limitless possibilities that awaited. The air was thin and cold, but the sense of shared purpose between the two visionaries created a warmth of its own.

"This is just the beginning," Musk said, his voice filled with determination and a hint of awe. He gazed out at the horizon, his mind racing with plans and dreams for the future. "With your help, we'll turn Mars into a second home for humanity." His words carried the weight of his commitment and the hope of millions who believed in the potential of human ingenuity and resilience.

Enki placed a hand on Musk's shoulder, a gesture of solidarity and support. "And we will be here to support you every step of the way. Our journey together has only just begun." Enki's voice was calm and reassuring, filled with the wisdom of his long-lived race and the excitement of forging a new chapter in interstellar cooperation. The bond between them was a testament to what could be achieved when different worlds united in pursuit of a common goal.

As the spacecraft lifted off, carrying the team and their valuable insights back to Earth, they left behind not just a planet, but a vision for the future. The ancient facilities of Mars had been unveiled, their secrets now a source of inspiration and innovation. The collaboration between humans and the

Anunnaki had shown what was possible when two civilizations came together, combining their strengths and learning from each other in the pursuit of progress and discovery.

The world awaited their return, eager to hear the stories and see the discoveries that would shape the next chapter of human history. News of their mission had already sparked widespread excitement and curiosity, with people from all walks of life looking forward to the new technologies and knowledge that would emerge from their findings. The secrets of Mars had been unlocked, revealing a legacy of ancient wisdom and technological prowess that promised to propel humanity into a new era of exploration.

As humanity and the Anunnaki continued their journey together, they were guided by the hope that understanding and unity would light the way forward. The shared vision of a future defined by knowledge, cooperation, and shared purpose was a powerful motivator, driving them to unlock the mysteries of the universe. The partnership between Earth and Nibiru was more than just an alliance; it was a beacon of what could be achieved through collaboration and mutual respect.

The return journey was filled with a sense of accomplishment and anticipation for the future. The team members reviewed their data, refined their plans, and prepared to share their findings with the broader scientific community. They knew that their work was just beginning, and that the discoveries they had made would pave the way for future missions and advancements.

The successful mission to Mars set a powerful precedent for future endeavors, reinforcing the potential of human and Anunnaki cooperation. It demonstrated that by working together, they could overcome the challenges of space exploration and unlock the vast potential of the cosmos. The vision of a thriving human colony on Mars was no longer a distant dream, but an attainable reality.

As the spacecraft approached Earth, the team felt a renewed sense of purpose and excitement. They were bringing back more than just data and artifacts; they were carrying the promise of a brighter future, one where humanity could expand its horizons and explore the wonders of the universe. The collaboration between Musk and the Anunnaki had shown that when two civilizations come together, they can achieve extraordinary things.

The world awaited their return, eager to hear the stories and see the discoveries that would shape the next chapter of human history. The mission to Mars had been a remarkable success, unlocking secrets that would inspire generations to come. As humanity and the Anunnaki continued their journey together, they were guided by the hope that understanding and unity would light the way forward, unlocking the mysteries of the universe and building a future defined by knowledge, cooperation, and shared purpose.

CHAPTER 8: CULTURAL EXCHANGE

As the Anunnaki began to integrate with human society, they found themselves captivated by the intricacies of modern culture. The vibrant and diverse expressions of art, fashion, music, and entertainment fascinated them. Each cultural nuance was a new discovery, and they immersed themselves in the richness of human creativity with childlike wonder and scholarly curiosity. They attended concerts where the pulsating rhythms and emotive performances of contemporary musicians left them mesmerized. They marveled at the skill and technique displayed by artists whose works hung in prestigious museums, each piece a testament to human innovation and imagination.

The Anunnaki also delved into the digital realms of social media and virtual reality, exploring platforms that offered endless streams of content and interaction. They were particularly struck by the way these technologies connected people across vast distances, creating communities and subcultures that transcended traditional boundaries. The immersion in virtual reality experiences allowed them to walk through historical reconstructions, attend virtual performances, and even interact with digital representations of people and places, providing a profound understanding of humanity's technological advancements.

The celebrities of the 21st century, with their beauty, charisma, and influence, particularly intrigued the Anunnaki. Figures like movie stars, musicians, and social media influencers embodied the pinnacle of human cultural achievements, and their lives were followed with avid interest. These celebrities were not just entertainers; they were icons who shaped public opinion, trends, and cultural values. The Anunnaki observed how a single post or appearance could sway millions, a phenomenon that resonated with their understanding of leadership and influence.

At public events and private gatherings, the Anunnaki mingled with human celebrities, learning about their lifestyles and the adoration they inspired among their fans. They attended film premieres, award ceremonies, and exclusive parties, where they engaged in conversations that ranged from the trivial to the profound. These interactions offered them insights into the human experience, from the pressures of fame to the impact of media and technology on personal and public life.

They were intrigued by the fame and influence these individuals wielded, seeing parallels with their own leaders and influential figures. Just as the Anunnaki had revered figures who guided their society, human celebrities played a pivotal role in shaping cultural narratives and aspirations. Enki, Lord Enlil, and Inanna often engaged in deep conversations with these modern icons, exchanging ideas and philosophies that spanned the millennia and the stars. They found common ground in their discussions about leadership, creativity, and the responsibilities that came with influence.

Enki, with his vast knowledge and experience, often discussed the parallels between ancient myths and modern storytelling, highlighting the enduring power of narrative to shape societies. Lord Enlil, with his strategic mind, explored the impact of celebrity culture on global politics and social movements, drawing connections between human history and the Anunnaki's own past. Inanna, known for her beauty and wisdom, found herself particularly drawn to the artistic expressions of humanity, engaging in conversations about the nature of beauty, fame, and the human condition.

Through these interactions, the Anunnaki gained a deeper

appreciation for the complexities and nuances of human culture. They saw how the arts and media could both reflect and shape societal values, acting as a mirror and a catalyst for change. The experience enriched their understanding of humanity, fostering a sense of connection and mutual respect. This cultural exchange was not just about observing and learning; it was about engaging and contributing to a shared future where both civilizations could benefit from each other's strengths and insights.

This fascination, however, led to misunderstandings. Some Anunnaki, influenced by their historical memories and ancient practices, believed they could claim human women as they had in ancient times. In their past, the Anunnaki had relationships with humans, often resulting in revered figures and demigods in various mythologies. These unions were celebrated in ancient texts and often viewed as divine blessings, giving rise to legendary heroes and influential leaders. Such historical precedents, combined with their admiration for human beauty and charm, led a few Anunnaki to assume that similar customs would still be acceptable in the modern era.

When a few Anunnaki began expressing their intentions to claim relationships with human women, it caused immediate concern and confusion. The public reactions were mixed, ranging from curiosity to outright outrage. Some people were intrigued by the idea of rekindling ancient bonds, seeing it as a romantic notion steeped in myth and legend. However, the majority of the public found the idea deeply unsettling. The notion of claiming another person as a partner without mutual consent was seen as archaic and unacceptable.

These assumptions were quickly challenged, as humanity had evolved beyond such practices. Modern societies emphasized autonomy, consent, and mutual respect in relationships, principles that were non-negotiable and foundational to contemporary social norms. The idea of personal freedom and the right to choose one's partner was deeply ingrained in human culture, and any violation of these principles was met with strong resistance.

The Anunnaki found themselves facing the complexities of modern human social norms and laws, which were far more nuanced than those of ancient times. They realized that their actions could easily be misinterpreted and cause harm, leading to a swift need for clarification and cultural sensitivity training. The misunderstandings highlighted the vast differences between ancient and modern customs, underscoring the importance of education and communication in bridging these gaps.

In response, diplomatic efforts were intensified to address the issue. Workshops and seminars on contemporary human social norms and ethics were organized, attended by both Anunnaki and human representatives. These sessions aimed to educate the Anunnaki on the principles of consent and respect that governed modern relationships, ensuring that they understood and respected these values. Human sociologists, anthropologists, and legal experts played a crucial role in these training programs, providing historical context and practical guidelines for navigating modern social interactions.

The Anunnaki leaders, including Enki, Lord Enlil, and Inanna, took these lessons to heart. They issued public statements acknowledging the misunderstandings and expressing their commitment to respecting human norms and values. Enki, in particular, emphasized the importance of learning and adapting, drawing parallels to the Anunnaki's own history of evolution and change. He urged his people to approach these new experiences with humility and openness, fostering a spirit of mutual respect and understanding.

This period of adjustment was challenging but ultimately fruitful. The Anunnaki's willingness to learn and adapt earned them respect and goodwill from many human communities. They demonstrated a genuine desire to integrate harmoniously into human society, showing that even ancient beings could embrace change and growth. This process of learning and adaptation strengthened the bonds between the two civilizations, paving the way for deeper and more meaningful exchanges in the future.

Diplomatic efforts were immediately initiated to address the misunderstandings. Recognizing the urgency and sensitivity of the situation, leaders from both Anunnaki and human communities came together in a series of high-level meetings to discuss and resolve the issues. These gatherings were held in prominent international venues, symbolizing the importance of the collaboration and the commitment to finding a harmonious solution. The atmosphere was one of mutual respect and a shared desire for understanding.

Enki, with his deep understanding of human history and culture, played a key role in these negotiations. His extensive knowledge of both civilizations positioned him as a bridge between the two worlds. During these discussions, he acknowledged the Anunnaki's missteps with humility and sincerity, stressing that their actions were based on ancient customs that no longer applied. Enki emphasized the importance of respecting human autonomy and choice, principles that are foundational in contemporary societies. His candidness and willingness to address the issues head-on were instrumental in building trust and fostering a constructive dialogue.

Public forums, educational workshops, and cultural exchange programs were established to foster better understanding between the two civilizations. These initiatives were designed to be comprehensive and inclusive, targeting various segments of society. Public forums provided a platform for open discussion, where people from all walks of life could voice their concerns, ask questions, and share their perspectives. These forums were moderated by experts in intercultural communication and conflict resolution, ensuring that the dialogue remained respectful and productive.

Educational workshops were tailored to different audiences, from schoolchildren to professionals. These workshops covered a range of topics, including the history of Anunnaki-human interactions, contemporary human values, and social norms. Participants engaged in interactive activities and simulations that helped them understand and empathize with the perspectives of the other civilization. These educational efforts were critical in dispelling myths and misconceptions, paving the way for mutual respect and cooperation.

Cultural exchange programs were another cornerstone of these diplomatic efforts. These programs facilitated the exchange of art, music, literature, and other cultural expressions between the Anunnaki and humans. Exhibitions showcased the rich heritage of both civilizations, while joint performances and collaborative projects highlighted the creative potential of their union. These cultural exchanges were not only enlightening but also served to humanize the Anunnaki and foster a sense of shared identity.

Inanna, known for her beauty and wisdom, took a leading role in these efforts. Her presence and influence were invaluable in bridging the gap between the two civilizations. Inanna spoke publicly about the importance of mutual respect and understanding, drawing on her own experiences and insights. Her speeches were eloquent and heartfelt, resonating deeply with audiences. She used her platform to advocate for peaceful and respectful interactions, highlighting the benefits of collaboration and unity.

Her public appearances were strategically planned to reach a wide audience. She participated in televised interviews, public rallies, and international conferences, consistently delivering a message of unity and cooperation. Inanna's charm and eloquence helped to ease tensions and build bridges of understanding. Her efforts were complemented by those of other Anunnaki and human leaders, creating a united front that underscored the commitment to a peaceful resolution.

The resolution of these misunderstandings was rooted in respecting human autonomy and choice. Recognizing the importance of these principles, leaders from both civilizations established a framework that emphasized consent and mutual interest. It was agreed that any interested women would have the option to visit Nibiru, provided they did so willingly and without coercion. This approach ensured that relationships were based on mutual consent and genuine interest, rather than outdated notions of claim and possession. It was a significant step towards aligning the Anunnaki's practices with contemporary human values, reflecting a profound respect for individual rights and freedoms.

To facilitate this process, comprehensive information sessions were held to inform interested individuals about Nibiru and what to expect if they chose to visit. These sessions covered various aspects of Anunnaki culture, daily life on Nibiru, and the logistics of travel and stay. Experts provided detailed presentations and answered questions, ensuring that participants had a clear understanding of what the experience would entail. The transparency of these sessions was crucial in building trust and ensuring that decisions were made with full knowledge and consideration.

The process was transparent and supportive, prioritizing the safety and well-being of those involved. Psychological and cultural counselors were made available to provide guidance and support, helping individuals navigate the complexities of intercultural relationships. Legal frameworks were also established to protect the rights of visitors, ensuring that their autonomy was respected at all times. This comprehensive support system was designed to create an environment where participants felt secure and valued.

The option to visit Nibiru became a symbol of the new,

respectful partnership between the Anunnaki and humanity, highlighting the progress made in their cultural exchange. It represented a shift from historical practices to modern values, demonstrating the Anunnaki's commitment to understanding and integrating human principles. This initiative was widely publicized and celebrated as a milestone in the evolving relationship between the two civilizations.

As the Anunnaki and humans continued to learn from each other, the initial misunderstandings gave way to deeper connections and shared experiences. Joint cultural festivals, collaborative art projects, and shared scientific endeavors became common, fostering a sense of unity and mutual appreciation. These interactions enriched both societies, allowing them to draw strength from their diversity and find common ground in their shared aspirations.

The cultural exchange became a foundation for a stronger, more unified future, where both civilizations could thrive together, guided by the principles of respect, autonomy, and mutual understanding. This new chapter in their relationship was not just about integrating technology and knowledge but also about building a society where diverse cultures and values could coexist harmoniously. It was about creating a world where the strengths and wisdom of each civilization could complement and enhance the other, leading to a more inclusive and enlightened future.

The collaborative spirit extended beyond mere coexistence, inspiring innovative solutions to common challenges and driving progress in various fields. By embracing each other's perspectives and learning from their respective histories, the Anunnaki and humans laid the groundwork for a partnership that was resilient, dynamic, and forward-looking. This alliance was a testament to what could be achieved when respect for individual rights and a commitment to mutual benefit guided interstellar relations.

CHAPTER 9: THE GOLD RUSH

The extraction of gold began in earnest, with the Anunnaki employing their advanced technology to expedite the process. Sophisticated machinery and techniques, far beyond current human capabilities, were deployed across the globe. Massive, gleaming extraction rigs, operating with precision and efficiency, tapped into previously inaccessible gold reserves. These towering structures, with their sleek, futuristic designs and automated systems, worked around the clock, ensuring a constant flow of precious metal. The Anunnaki's methods minimized environmental impact, using clean energy sources and advanced filtration systems to ensure sustainability. Solar and geothermal energy powered the operations, while innovative water purification and waste management systems protected local ecosystems from contamination and disruption.

Enki oversaw the operations, coordinating with both Anunnaki engineers and human scientists. His leadership was instrumental in ensuring that the process was smooth and efficient. Under his guidance, teams of experts from both civilizations worked in unison, sharing knowledge and skills. Anunnaki engineers brought their unparalleled technological expertise, while human scientists contributed their understanding of local geological conditions and environmental factors. This collaboration fostered a sense of camaraderie and mutual respect, as both groups learned from each other and strived towards a common goal.

The extraction sites, scattered across continents, became hubs of frenetic activity. From the deserts of Africa to the rainforests of South America, these sites were bustling with the energy and excitement of discovery. The machinery, with its constant hum and rhythmic movements, created a symphony of industrial progress. Workers moved with purpose, their efforts coordinated through sophisticated communication networks that ensured every aspect of the operation was meticulously managed.

Despite the monumental scale of the operations, the Anunnaki maintained strict adherence to safety and ecological standards, reflecting their deep respect for Earth and its inhabitants. They implemented rigorous safety protocols, ensuring that all personnel were protected from potential hazards. Regular inspections and maintenance routines kept the machinery in optimal condition, preventing accidents and breakdowns. Environmental monitoring systems were in place to track the impact of the extraction process, allowing for quick adjustments to mitigate any negative effects.

The sight of these towering machines and the relentless pace of gold extraction was both awe-inspiring and unsettling. For the first time, humanity witnessed the full extent of Anunnaki technological prowess, a blend of efficiency and power that seemed almost magical. The machines moved with a grace and precision that defied their massive size, performing tasks that would have taken human technology decades to accomplish. This display of advanced engineering left many observers in a state of wonder, contemplating the possibilities that such technology could unlock for the future.

The process, though beneficial in many ways, also highlighted the vast technological gap between the two civilizations. While the Anunnaki's methods were efficient and environmentally friendly, they were also a stark reminder of how far humanity had yet to go. This realization sparked a range of reactions, from admiration and aspiration to feelings of inadequacy and dependence. However, it also served as a catalyst for innovation, inspiring human scientists and engineers to push the boundaries of their own capabilities in an effort to bridge this gap.

In the midst of these operations, the Anunnaki's presence became a symbol of progress and potential. Their advanced technology and respectful approach to resource extraction set a new standard for how such processes could be conducted. The collaboration between Anunnaki and humans at these sites exemplified the possibilities of what could be achieved when two advanced civilizations worked together towards a common goal. The extraction of gold, once a purely economic activity, had transformed into a beacon of technological advancement and environmental stewardship, paving the way for a future where such practices could become the norm rather than the exception.

This sudden depletion of the precious metal caused significant unrest among the world's elite, who saw their wealth diminish. Gold, long a symbol of power and economic stability, was now being siphoned off at an unprecedented rate. The global markets reacted with volatility, and the value of gold fluctuated wildly. Investors and financial institutions, who had relied on the steady value of gold as a bedrock of economic security, were now facing uncharted waters. Panic spread through the trading floors as the stability they had depended on began to crumble.

The wealthy, who had hoarded gold as a secure investment, found themselves facing unexpected financial uncertainty. These elites, accustomed to the predictability and safety that gold had historically provided, were suddenly confronted with the reality that their once-solid assets were dwindling. Their financial portfolios, heavily weighted with gold, were rapidly devaluing, threatening their economic dominance and lifestyle.

Protests erupted in financial districts around the world, with influential figures and organizations demanding a halt to the extraction. High-profile demonstrations took place outside stock exchanges, central banks, and government buildings. Protesters, many of whom were prominent financiers and business leaders, carried placards and gave impassioned speeches. They argued that the rapid depletion of gold reserves threatened the global economy and undermined their financial security. The once-quiet corridors of financial power were now filled with angry voices and urgent demands.

Media outlets amplified these concerns, creating a climate of fear and anxiety. News channels ran 24-hour coverage on the "Gold Crisis," featuring expert panels debating the long-term impacts on global markets. Headlines screamed of impending economic collapse, and social media buzzed with speculation and alarm. The uncertainty permeated all levels of society, from small investors to multinational corporations, creating a pervasive sense of instability.

Governments were caught in a difficult position, needing to balance the demands of their wealthy constituents with the broader benefits that the Anunnaki partnership promised. Political leaders faced intense pressure from powerful lobbying groups and influential donors who insisted that the gold extraction be halted immediately. At the same time, they were acutely aware of the transformative potential of the Anunnaki's technological and scientific contributions.

Intense negotiations ensued, with the Anunnaki reassuring world leaders that their contributions to human advancement far outweighed the temporary economic disruptions. High-level diplomatic meetings were convened, where Enki and other Anunnaki representatives presented detailed plans for mitigating the economic impact. They offered to share advanced technologies that could revitalize other sectors of the economy, promising innovations in energy, healthcare, and infrastructure that would more than compensate for the loss of gold.

These discussions were complex and fraught with tension. Economic advisors and financial experts pored over projections and impact assessments, weighing the immediate losses against the potential long-term gains. The Anunnaki's calm and methodical approach helped to allay some fears, but the negotiations required careful diplomacy and significant concessions on both sides.

In the end, a tentative agreement was reached, balancing the need for economic stability with the extraordinary opportunities presented by the Anunnaki alliance. The world's elite, though still apprehensive, began to adjust their strategies, looking for new investment opportunities in the emerging technologies and industries that the Anunnaki were helping to develop. The broader population, meanwhile, watched closely, hopeful that the promised advancements would lead to a brighter and more prosperous future.

The global economy remained volatile, but the intense focus on innovation and collaboration sparked a renewed sense of purpose. The unrest among the elite highlighted the challenges of navigating such a profound shift, but it also underscored the resilience and adaptability of human societies. As the world moved forward, the lessons learned from this period of turmoil would shape the evolving partnership between humanity and the Anunnaki, paving the way for a future defined by cooperation and shared progress.

Despite the turmoil, the majority of humanity welcomed the Anunnaki's gifts. The advances in medicine, energy, and transportation began to transform societies on a global scale, ushering in a new era of prosperity. The Anunnaki introduced revolutionary medical technologies that eradicated diseases previously thought incurable. Lifesaving treatments and regenerative therapies became widely available, significantly increasing life expectancy and quality of life. Hospitals were equipped with advanced diagnostic tools and treatment methods, enabling doctors to tackle illnesses with unprecedented precision and effectiveness. Chronic conditions that had plagued humanity for centuries were now manageable or entirely curable, reducing suffering and healthcare costs dramatically.

In the energy sector, the Anunnaki shared sustainable technologies that harnessed solar, geothermal, and other renewable resources with unparalleled efficiency. New energy grids were constructed using cutting-edge materials and designs, drastically reducing energy loss and improving distribution. Dependency on fossil fuels plummeted, mitigating the impacts of climate change and contributing to a cleaner, healthier environment. These innovations provided clean, abundant energy to even the most remote regions, fostering economic growth and improving living standards. Communities that had been off the grid now had access to reliable power, fueling education, business, and technological development.

Transportation was also revolutionized. The Anunnaki's advanced propulsion systems and anti-gravity technologies made long-distance travel faster, safer, and more affordable. Hyperloop networks, powered by clean energy, connected cities and countries in ways that were previously unimaginable. These high-speed transit systems cut travel times drastically, making daily commutes across countries a reality. Air travel evolved with the introduction of anti-gravity vehicles, which were not only faster but also more environmentally friendly and less reliant on conventional airports.

Space travel, once the domain of a select few, became accessible to ordinary people, opening new frontiers for exploration and commerce. Spaceports sprang up around the world, and civilian space flights became as routine as airplane travel. The prospect of colonizing other planets or simply vacationing in space became realistic goals. These advancements sparked a new age of exploration, reigniting the human spirit of adventure and discovery.

The overall impact of the Anunnaki's gifts was transformative.

Societies that had struggled with poverty, disease, and energy scarcity experienced unprecedented growth and stability. Education systems were overhauled to include Anunnaki knowledge, preparing future generations to thrive in a rapidly advancing world. Schools and universities introduced new curricula that incorporated advanced sciences, interstellar navigation, and ethical considerations of technological use. Students were inspired by the possibilities of the future, equipped with the skills and knowledge to harness the advancements they inherited.

The initial unrest and resistance faded as the tangible benefits of the Anunnaki partnership became apparent. Communities that had been skeptical or resistant to change found themselves thriving under the new technologies and opportunities. The elite, though still adjusting to the new economic realities, found new opportunities in the evolving markets and technologies. They began to invest in the burgeoning industries of space travel, renewable energy, and biotech, capitalizing on the new economic landscape.

The broader population, empowered by improved health, education, and opportunities, embraced the changes with optimism and enthusiasm. Cities became hubs of innovation and cultural exchange, drawing inspiration from both human ingenuity and Anunnaki wisdom. The improvements in quality of life fostered a renewed sense of global unity and purpose, as people from diverse backgrounds worked together to build a brighter future.

CHAPTER 10: ENKI'S VISION

Lord Enki, ever the visionary, gathered leaders and thinkers from around the world to share his dream of a unified Earth, free from the divisions that had plagued humanity for millennia. The grand assembly was held at the newly established interstellar council headquarters, a magnificent structure that symbolized the dawn of a new era. The headquarters itself was an architectural marvel, combining elements of human and Anunnaki design to create a space that embodied harmony and cooperation. The building's soaring towers and vast halls were filled with light, reflecting the openness and transparency that Enki championed.

As Enki stood before a diverse audience of politicians, scientists, cultural icons, and everyday citizens, his presence commanded respect, and his words resonated deeply. The room was filled with an air of anticipation and hope, as the attendees knew they were witnessing a pivotal moment in history.

"Throughout your history," Enki began, his voice both powerful and gentle, "humanity has faced countless challenges and conflicts. These divisions, rooted in race, religion, nationality, and ideology, have hindered your progress and caused immense suffering. But now, we stand at the threshold of a new era, one where the possibilities are limitless if we can come together as one."

The audience was silent, hanging on his every word. Enki's vision was not just about technological advancement but about social and spiritual evolution. His words painted a picture of a future where humanity had transcended its differences to build a society based on mutual respect and shared values.

"Imagine a world where resources are shared equitably," he continued, his voice imbued with passion and conviction, "where education and healthcare are accessible to all, and where environmental stewardship is a priority. A world united in its efforts to explore the cosmos, with humans joining the Anunnaki in our quest for knowledge and understanding."

He paused, letting his words sink in. The silence in the room was profound, as everyone absorbed the magnitude of his vision. "The stars are not just for the few," he proclaimed, his eyes reflecting the vastness of space. "They are for all of us, and together we can reach them."

The room remained hushed, the gravity of his words leaving a lasting impact on all who heard them. One of the politicians in the audience raised his hand, a look of earnest curiosity on his face. "Lord Enki, how do you propose we overcome the deeply rooted divisions that have existed for so long?"

Enki smiled warmly, his demeanor radiating compassion and wisdom. "By fostering a culture of empathy, education, and cooperation," he responded. "We must focus on our shared humanity and the common goals that unite us. The journey will not be easy, but it is necessary for the survival and prosperity of our species."

He continued, "Empathy will help us understand each other's struggles and perspectives. Education will equip us with the knowledge and skills to address our challenges. Cooperation will enable us to pool our resources and strengths to achieve our common goals."

As Enki spoke, holographic images appeared around him, illustrating his points with vivid clarity. Scenes of diverse groups working together on scientific projects, communities rebuilding after natural disasters, and joint human-Anunnaki explorations of distant planets filled the room. These visual aids reinforced his message, showing the tangible benefits of unity and collaboration.

"Together, we can create a future where every individual has the opportunity to thrive," Enki concluded. "A future where we look to the stars not as isolated nations, but as a united Earth, ready to embrace the infinite possibilities of the cosmos."

The audience erupted into applause, the sound echoing through the grand hall. The vision Enki had shared was both inspiring and attainable, a beacon of hope for a world weary of division and conflict. As the applause died down, the attendees knew that they had been given a glimpse of a brighter future, one that they were now committed to making a reality.

Jordan Peterson, with his profound understanding of psychology and human behavior, played a pivotal role in promoting Enki's vision. Recognizing the immense potential of this transformative period, Peterson dedicated himself to bridging the gap between ancient wisdom and modern knowledge. He traveled extensively, speaking at universities, international forums, and public gatherings. His itinerary included visits to cities across continents, each stop marked by a new audience eager to hear his insights. His message was clear and compelling: humanity must transcend its historical divisions and embrace a collective identity.

At a conference in Geneva, Peterson addressed a packed auditorium. The venue was filled with scholars, policymakers, students, and professionals, all drawn by the promise of new perspectives. The atmosphere was charged with anticipation as Peterson took the stage. "We have always sought to understand our place in the universe," he began, his voice resonating with conviction. "Now, we have an unprecedented opportunity to define that place through unity and shared purpose. Lord Enki's vision challenges us to think beyond our immediate concerns and to embrace a global perspective."

His words struck a chord with the audience. The notion of a unified humanity, working together towards common goals, was both inspiring and daunting. During a panel discussion that followed, a young student from the audience raised a hand and asked, "Dr. Peterson, how can we, as individuals, contribute to this grand vision?"

Peterson leaned forward, his expression earnest and engaging. "By educating ourselves and others," he replied, "by fostering dialogue and understanding, and by being active participants in our communities. Each of us has a role to play in building this unified future." His eyes scanned the room, ensuring that his message was received by all. "It's not just about grand gestures or sweeping reforms. It's about the small, everyday actions that collectively make a significant impact. We need to be proactive in learning, teaching, and engaging with those around us."

He advocated for educational reforms that emphasized critical thinking, empathy, and global citizenship. "We must nurture these values in young people," he urged, "so that future generations are better equipped to navigate and overcome the challenges of a diverse and interconnected world." He spoke passionately about the importance of developing curricula that included not just academic knowledge, but also lessons on emotional intelligence and ethical responsibility. "Education should not just be about preparing for a career," he said, "but about preparing for life as a thoughtful, compassionate, and active member of a global society."

Peterson's talks often included practical examples and actionable steps that individuals could take. He encouraged his listeners to engage in community service, participate in cultural exchanges, and use technology to connect with people from different backgrounds. "In our interconnected world," he said, "we have the tools to build bridges rather than walls. Use social media to start meaningful conversations, volunteer in multicultural settings, and always seek to learn from those who are different from you."

Through his efforts, Peterson helped shift public perception. His influence was instrumental in creating a groundswell of support for Enki's vision. People began to see themselves not just as citizens of their respective countries but as members of a global community with a shared destiny. His speeches were often followed by lively discussions, workshops, and community projects aimed at implementing the ideas he championed.

Peterson's advocacy extended beyond public speaking. He collaborated with educational institutions to develop new programs, advised governments on policy reforms, and worked with NGOs to promote cross-cultural understanding. His multifaceted approach ensured that the message of unity and collective identity reached a wide audience and had a lasting impact.

The changes in public perception were palpable. Schools started adopting more inclusive curricula, communities launched initiatives to promote intercultural dialogue, and policymakers began considering global implications in their decisions. Peterson's work had ignited a movement that aligned with Enki's vision, paving the way for a future where humanity could overcome its divisions and thrive as a united force in the cosmos.

Graham Hancock, with his extensive knowledge of ancient civilizations and their interconnectedness, became a key advocate for Enki's vision of global cooperation and understanding. Drawing upon decades of research and exploration, Hancock's work provided a profound insight into how ancient cultures once thrived through mutual respect and collaboration. He wrote extensively on the subject, drawing on historical parallels to illustrate the benefits of unity. His books and articles became bestsellers, resonating with a wide audience and sparking a global conversation about humanity's shared heritage and future.

Hancock's writings were not mere academic treatises but

compelling narratives that connected the dots between past and present. His eloquent prose and vivid descriptions brought to life the stories of ancient peoples who had achieved remarkable feats through cooperative efforts. These stories highlighted the achievements of civilizations like the Sumerians, Egyptians, and the Maya, whose successes in architecture, governance, and science were often the result of cross-cultural exchanges and alliances.

At a cultural symposium in Cairo, Hancock addressed an audience of scholars and cultural leaders. The historic venue, imbued with the legacy of Egypt's grand history, was the perfect backdrop for his impassioned speech. "Our ancestors understood the importance of collaboration," he said, his voice resonating with conviction. "It's time we rediscover that wisdom and apply it to our modern world. The Anunnaki have shown us what is possible when we work together."

The audience listened intently as Hancock detailed the ways in which ancient civilizations had benefited from mutual learning and cooperation. He emphasized the idea that, just as the Anunnaki had integrated their advanced knowledge with Earth's early cultures, modern societies could achieve unprecedented progress through global collaboration.

Hancock organized and participated in numerous cultural exchange programs, bringing together scholars, artists, and community leaders from different backgrounds. These programs highlighted the common threads that linked disparate cultures, fostering a sense of shared identity and mutual respect. "Our cultural diversity is our strength," Hancock often said during these exchanges. "By celebrating our differences and finding common ground, we can build a more united and prosperous world."

These cultural exchanges were more than symbolic gestures; they involved practical collaborations that produced tangible results. Workshops, joint research projects, and collaborative art installations were just some of the initiatives that emerged from these programs. Participants from various cultural backgrounds worked together, sharing their knowledge and skills, and in the process, they built lasting relationships and understanding.

During a televised interview, the host asked, "Mr. Hancock, how do we balance the preservation of cultural identities with the push for global unity?" Hancock responded thoughtfully, "By recognizing that unity does not mean uniformity. We can honor and preserve our unique cultural identities while working towards common goals. It's about creating a tapestry where each thread is distinct yet contributes to the overall beauty and strength of the fabric."

Hancock's message was clear: global unity did not require the erasure of individual cultural identities. Instead, it called for a celebration of diversity within a framework of shared values and objectives. He often used metaphors and historical analogies to illustrate this point, making his arguments both accessible and compelling to a broad audience.

Together, Peterson and Hancock's efforts complemented Enki's vision, providing the intellectual and cultural foundations necessary for a unified Earth. They worked tirelessly to build bridges between communities, foster dialogue, and promote the values of empathy, cooperation, and shared destiny. Their combined influence extended beyond academia and cultural circles into the hearts and minds of ordinary people around the world.

As the world began to embrace these ideals, the potential for humanity to join the Anunnaki in exploring the cosmos grew ever closer to reality. The collaborative spirit that Enki, Peterson, and Hancock championed set the stage for a future where divisions were overcome, and a unified Earth could reach for the stars. Their vision inspired a generation to look beyond borders and differences, to see the potential of a united human race venturing forth into the universe together. This new era, built on the principles of shared knowledge and mutual respect, promised to transform not only human society but also its place in the cosmos.

CHAPTER 11: CHALLENGES AND TRIUMPHS

The integration of Anunnaki technology was not without its challenges. Despite the promise of a brighter future, the early days were marked by a series of accidents and setbacks as humanity struggled to adapt to the new advancements. In laboratories and factories around the world, scientists and engineers grappled with technologies that were often decades, if not centuries, ahead of human understanding. The complexity of the Anunnaki devices was astounding, and each new piece of equipment presented unique and unforeseen difficulties.

In a high-tech laboratory in Silicon Valley, a team of engineers worked tirelessly to reverse-engineer Anunnaki propulsion systems. The lab was filled with advanced machinery and computer systems, each station buzzing with activity. Despite their best efforts, progress was slow and fraught with difficulties. The engineers, accustomed to pushing the boundaries of innovation, found themselves repeatedly confounded by the alien technology.

One afternoon, as they attempted to test a newly assembled prototype, the machinery sparked violently, sending a shower of sparks and smoke into the air. Alarms blared, and the room was quickly filled with the acrid smell of burning circuits.

"Shut it down! Shut it down now!" shouted Dr. Maria Alvarez, the lead engineer, as she rushed to the control panel. The team scrambled to power down the equipment, their faces pale with fear and frustration. The cacophony of malfunctioning machines was deafening, and the tension in the room was palpable.

Once the immediate danger had passed, Dr. Alvarez gathered her team in the conference room adjacent to the lab. The walls were lined with whiteboards covered in complex diagrams and equations, testament to the team's relentless efforts. The engineers sat in silence, their expressions a mix of exhaustion and disappointment.

"We knew this wouldn't be easy," Dr. Alvarez began, her voice steady but firm. "But we can't let these setbacks discourage us. Each failure brings us one step closer to success. We need to learn from these mistakes and keep pushing forward." Her eyes scanned the room, making contact with each team member, conveying both determination and empathy.

Her words resonated with the team. They nodded in agreement, their resolve strengthened. They knew the road ahead would be difficult, but they were determined to overcome the obstacles and unlock the secrets of Anunnaki technology. The incident had shaken them, but it also reinforced their commitment to the task at hand. They understood that they were pioneers on the frontier of a new technological era, and that their perseverance was crucial for humanity's future.

The team returned to their workstations with renewed vigor. They re-examined their data, adjusted their models, and brainstormed new approaches. Collaboration became their greatest asset, as they drew on each other's strengths and insights to solve the complex problems before them. The laboratory, once filled with the noise of malfunctioning machinery, was now alive with the quiet hum of focused activity and the buzz of collaborative discussions.

Meanwhile, similar scenes played out in other research centers around the globe. In Geneva, medical researchers faced their own set of challenges as they worked to integrate Anunnaki regenerative therapies into human medicine. In Tokyo, engineers strove to apply Anunnaki energy solutions to modern power grids. Each team faced setbacks and frustrations, but they also shared a collective determination to succeed.

Dr. Alvarez's team in Silicon Valley eventually made significant progress. After months of trial and error, they managed to stabilize the prototype propulsion system. The breakthrough was met with a mix of relief and excitement. As the prototype hummed steadily, displaying the first signs of reliable function, the team erupted into cheers. This success was not just a technological milestone; it was a testament to their resilience and ingenuity.

The initial struggles with Anunnaki technology underscored the vast gap between human and alien knowledge. Yet, it also highlighted the incredible capacity for human innovation and adaptability. As the teams around the world continued their work, they moved closer to a future where the integration of Anunnaki advancements would bring about unprecedented progress and prosperity for all of humanity.

In another part of the world, a group of medical researchers faced their own set of challenges. At a leading research hospital in Geneva, doctors and scientists were working to integrate Anunnaki regenerative therapies into human medicine. The potential to cure previously untreatable diseases was within reach, but the complexity of the technology posed significant hurdles. The research facility was a hub of activity, filled with the latest medical equipment and a team of experts from various fields, all driven by the shared goal of transforming healthcare.

Dr. Hassan Rahman, a renowned neurosurgeon, stood before a group of his colleagues, reviewing the latest data. The room was lined with screens displaying intricate diagrams of human and Anunnaki cellular structures, along with sequences of DNA and protein synthesis pathways. "We've made some progress, but there are still too many variables we don't fully understand," he explained, pointing to the complex biochemical pathways on the screen. "The Anunnaki's regenerative processes are fundamentally different from our own. Their cells have a remarkable ability to repair and renew, but the mechanisms behind this are still a mystery to us. We need to find a way to bridge that gap."

One of the younger researchers, Dr. Emily Carter, raised her hand. "What if we focus on the similarities first?" she suggested, her eyes bright with enthusiasm. "If we can identify the commonalities between our biology and theirs, it might give us a foundation to build on." Her proposal was met with murmurs of agreement from the rest of the team.

Dr. Rahman nodded thoughtfully, appreciating her fresh perspective. "That's a good approach, Emily. Let's reframe our research to identify those key similarities. It's time we start thinking outside the box. By understanding the fundamental biological processes that we share with the Anunnaki, we can develop hybrid treatments that are compatible with human physiology."

The team delved deeper into their research with renewed focus. They began cross-referencing human and Anunnaki genetic data, searching for genetic markers and molecular pathways that were conserved across both species. This comparative approach required meticulous analysis and a willingness to explore unconventional hypotheses. The researchers worked long hours, often late into the night, driven by the hope of achieving groundbreaking medical advancements.

Despite their dedication, the team faced numerous setbacks. There were moments of frustration and doubt as experiments failed and data proved inconclusive. The complexity of the Anunnaki technology, combined with the inherent differences between the two species, often seemed insurmountable. The researchers had to contend with unexpected side effects in their trial subjects, and some therapies that showed promise in theory proved unviable in practice.

During one particularly challenging week, the team experienced a series of disappointing results. Morale was low, and doubts began to surface. Dr. Rahman called an impromptu meeting to address the growing frustration. "I know this is difficult," he began, his tone serious but encouraging. "Innovation doesn't come without challenges. Every setback we face is an opportunity to learn and refine our approach. Remember, we're pioneers in this field. We are charting new territory, and that requires patience and perseverance."

His words reignited a spark of determination within the team. They returned to their workstations with a renewed sense of purpose, meticulously analyzing the data from their failed experiments to identify patterns and insights that could guide their next steps.

Slowly but surely, the collective determination to overcome these obstacles led to unprecedented innovation. The researchers discovered a set of regulatory genes that played a crucial role in both human and Anunnaki cell regeneration. By isolating these genes and understanding their function, the team was able to develop a prototype therapy that showed significant promise in early trials.

One evening, after a particularly successful series of tests, Dr. Carter approached Dr. Rahman. "We've done it," she said, her voice barely containing her excitement. "We've found a way to activate regenerative pathways in human cells without causing adverse reactions."

Dr. Rahman reviewed the results, a smile spreading across his face. "This is incredible, Emily. We've made a real breakthrough here. Let's prepare for the next phase of trials."

The breakthrough was met with cautious optimism. The researchers knew there was still a long road ahead, but the progress they had made was a testament to their hard work and innovative thinking. The integration of Anunnaki regenerative therapies into human medicine was no longer a distant dream, but a tangible reality within their grasp.

As word of their success spread, other research teams around the world were inspired to pursue similar paths of innovation and collaboration. The challenges faced by Dr. Rahman and his team underscored the difficulties of integrating alien technology, but their triumphs highlighted the incredible potential for progress when humanity's ingenuity is combined with Anunnaki advancements.

Despite the initial struggles, the collective efforts of humanity led to unprecedented innovation. The challenges encountered during the integration of Anunnaki technology served as catalysts for creativity and determination across various fields. In energy production, transportation, healthcare, and more, the fusion of human ingenuity and Anunnaki advancements began to yield remarkable results.

In fields ranging from energy production to transportation, the integration of Anunnaki technology began to yield remarkable results. Solar power plants equipped with Anunnaki enhancements operated at unparalleled efficiency, providing clean energy to millions. These plants utilized advanced photovoltaic materials and energy storage systems that drastically reduced energy loss and increased output. The impact was profound: entire regions that had previously struggled with energy shortages now enjoyed stable and sustainable power supplies. Cities gleamed with a new vibrancy as they harnessed this limitless, clean energy, driving economic growth and improving the quality of life.

In the realm of transportation, anti-gravity vehicles started to become a reality, revolutionizing the way people traveled. These vehicles, a marvel of engineering, combined Anunnaki levitation technology with cutting-edge human design. In a bustling workshop in Tokyo, a team of engineers gathered around a sleek, newly designed anti-gravity vehicle. Among them was Kenji Tanaka, a visionary engineer who had dedicated his career to making this technology accessible to the public.

The workshop buzzed with excitement as final preparations were made for the first public demonstration. Engineers checked and rechecked every component, ensuring everything was perfect. The vehicle itself, a gleaming masterpiece of aerodynamics and advanced materials, represented years of hard work and relentless pursuit of perfection.

As they prepared for the first public demonstration, Kenji addressed his team. His voice, filled with pride and anticipation, echoed through the workshop. "We've come a long way since we started this journey. Today, we show the world what's possible when we embrace new ideas and push beyond our limits."

The vehicle hovered gracefully above the ground, its sleek design a testament to the successful fusion of human ingenuity and Anunnaki technology. The demonstration took place in a large open plaza, surrounded by spectators and media. As the vehicle lifted off the ground, it moved effortlessly through the air, performing a series of maneuvers that left the crowd in awe. Its silent, smooth motion contrasted sharply with the noise and pollution of traditional vehicles, highlighting the revolutionary potential of this new technology.

The crowd that had gathered watched in awe as the vehicle moved effortlessly through the air. Cheers erupted, and cameras flashed, capturing the historic moment. Among the spectators were government officials, potential investors, and curious citizens, all witnessing the dawn of a new era in transportation.

After the demonstration, a journalist approached Kenji, eager to capture his thoughts on the groundbreaking achievement. "Mr. Tanaka, what do you think has been the most significant factor in overcoming the challenges you've faced?"

Kenji smiled, his eyes reflecting both the struggles and triumphs of the journey. "Collaboration," he replied. "Working together, sharing knowledge, and supporting each other. That's how we've been able to achieve what we have today. And it's how we'll continue to innovate and grow in the future."

His words resonated with the audience, embodying the spirit of unity and cooperation that had driven their success. The journey had not been easy, but it had shown that when humanity comes together, it can achieve the extraordinary.

The demonstration was a turning point. Governments and private companies alike began investing heavily in anti-gravity technology, envisioning a future where traffic jams and fossil fuels were relics of the past. The success of Kenji's team inspired others around the world to pursue similar innovations, sparking a global movement towards cleaner, more efficient transportation.

This collective drive towards innovation extended beyond transportation. In healthcare, Anunnaki medical technologies were adapted to create advanced diagnostic tools and treatments. Hospitals saw significant improvements in patient outcomes as new therapies for previously incurable diseases became available. Education systems incorporated Anunnaki knowledge, preparing students to thrive in an increasingly advanced and interconnected world.

The integration of Anunnaki technology had indeed led to unprecedented innovation. The world was on the brink of a new era, characterized by rapid advancements and boundless possibilities. The early struggles were now seen as necessary steps on the path to progress, each challenge met with determination and ingenuity. The collaborative spirit fostered during these efforts laid a strong foundation for future achievements, demonstrating that by working together, humanity could overcome any obstacle and reach new heights.

CHAPTER 12: THE MARS COLONY

With the Anunnaki's assistance, Elon Musk's dream of a Mars colony became a reality. The journey was long and arduous, filled with countless hours of preparation, training, and anticipation, but the promise of a new beginning on the red planet filled the pioneers with determination and excitement. The spacecraft, a marvel of combined human and Anunnaki engineering, hurtled through the void of space with an efficiency and speed previously unimaginable. As they approached Mars, the settlers could see the planet growing larger, its rusty hues a stark contrast against the blackness of space.

The first settlers, a diverse group of scientists, engineers, and adventurers, arrived on Mars aboard advanced spacecraft equipped with both human and Anunnaki technology. These pioneers represented the best of humanity's skills and spirit, ready to face the challenges of establishing a new home on an alien world. They were united by a common goal and the thrill of being the first humans to set foot on Mars.

As the landing craft touched down with a gentle thud, the settlers gazed out at the vast, dusty landscape through their viewport. The sky was a soft pink, and the horizon stretched endlessly, offering a sense of both isolation and limitless possibility. The Martian surface was a canvas of reddish soil, punctuated by the occasional rock formation or distant mountain range, all under the expansive, pastel-colored sky.

Elon Musk stood among the first to disembark, his face alight with a mixture of awe and pride. The airlock hissed open, and the settlers descended the ramp, their boots making the first human imprints on the Martian soil. The significance of the moment was not lost on anyone. They were pioneers, trailblazers of a new era. Musk took a deep breath, feeling the weight of history on his shoulders.

"Welcome to Mars," he announced, his voice carrying through the communication devices embedded in their suits. His words echoed through the crisp Martian air, filled with the promise of new beginnings. "This is the beginning of a new chapter for humanity. Let's get to work."

Dr. Sarah Zhang, the chief scientist of the expedition, approached Musk as they surveyed their surroundings. She held a tablet displaying the latest scan results from their orbital survey. "Elon, the initial scans show that the abandoned Anunnaki facilities are just a few kilometers from here," she said, her eyes sparkling with excitement. "We should set up a temporary base and then move our equipment there."

Musk nodded, his mind already racing with plans. The potential of what they might find in the Anunnaki facilities was enormous. "Agreed. Let's mobilize the team and start moving. The sooner we get to those facilities, the better."

The settlers began unloading their supplies and setting up temporary shelters. The landing site quickly transformed into a hive of activity. Modular habitats, powered by solar panels and equipped with life support systems, were assembled with precision and efficiency. The sense of camaraderie and shared purpose was palpable as they worked side by side. Conversations buzzed with excitement as they speculated about what they might find in the ancient structures and how they could adapt them for human use.

As they toiled, the settlers couldn't help but marvel at their surroundings. Mars, a planet once considered inhospitable, was becoming their new home. They were filled with a sense of accomplishment and the thrill of adventure. Each task, whether it was setting up a communications array or unpacking scientific equipment, brought them one step closer to realizing Musk's vision of a thriving Martian colony.

In the evenings, under the vast expanse of the Martian sky, the settlers would gather around their temporary habitats, sharing stories and dreams of the future. The challenges ahead were immense, but so was their resolve. They were united by a common goal and the knowledge that they were part of something much larger than themselves. As the first stars began to twinkle in the thin Martian atmosphere, the settlers looked to the horizon with hope and determination, ready to build a new world on the red planet.

The abandoned facilities proved invaluable, providing shelter and resources for the pioneers. Built into the Martian landscape, the structures were massive and intricately designed, a testament to the advanced engineering of the Anunnaki. The architecture blended seamlessly with the rocky terrain, making the buildings appear as if they had naturally emerged from the planet's surface. The structures were made of materials that seemed to possess self-healing properties, their surfaces smooth and unblemished despite the passage of millennia.

The settlers, equipped with advanced tools and protective suits, ventured into the depths of these ancient buildings with a mix of caution and curiosity. The air inside was still and cool, preserved by the airtight seals that had kept the Martian dust at bay. Dr. Sarah Zhang led the exploration team, her flashlight cutting through the darkness as they moved through the labyrinthine corridors. Each step echoed softly, amplifying the sense of mystery and wonder.

"These walls are made of materials we haven't even begun to understand," she marveled, running her gloved hand along the smooth surface. The walls seemed to absorb light, giving off a faint, otherworldly glow. "It's incredible how well-preserved everything is," she added, her voice filled with awe. The walls were adorned with intricate patterns and symbols, etched with a precision that defied human technology.

Elon Musk joined her, examining the strange symbols etched into the walls. "We need to document everything. This place is a goldmine of knowledge and technology," he said, his eyes scanning the intricate carvings. The symbols appeared to be part of a complex language, perhaps a blend of mathematics and art, hinting at the advanced intellect of the Anunnaki.

As they moved deeper into the facility, they discovered rooms filled with dormant machinery, strange artifacts, and what appeared to be data storage devices. The machinery was unlike anything they had seen before, with organic curves and metallic surfaces that seemed to pulse with latent energy. The artifacts ranged from small, handheld devices to large, immovable structures that hummed softly when approached.

The team worked meticulously, cataloging their findings and setting up research stations to begin decoding the Anunnaki technology. Dr. Zhang led the efforts with an unwavering focus, her team using a combination of human and Anunnaki tools to unlock the secrets hidden within the ancient machines. They recorded every detail, from the faint hum of the dormant machines to the intricate designs of the artifacts.

One evening, as the team gathered around a central control panel, Dr. Zhang's assistant, Alex, managed to activate a holographic interface. The room filled with a soft blue light as ancient schematics and maps appeared in the air. The holograms floated gently, casting an ethereal glow on the excited faces of the team.

"Look at this," Alex said excitedly, his fingers dancing over the holographic controls. "These are blueprints for the facility. It seems like there are sections dedicated to energy production, life support, and even agricultural development." The blueprints were incredibly detailed, showing layers of infrastructure that indicated a level of planning and foresight far beyond current human capabilities.

Musk studied the holograms, a grin spreading across his face. "This changes everything. We can use this technology to make Mars not just habitable, but thriving." The potential applications of the Anunnaki technology were staggering. Energy production systems that could harness the harsh Martian environment, life support systems capable of sustaining human life indefinitely, and agricultural technologies that could turn the barren landscape into fertile ground.

As the team continued their work, the sense of discovery and possibility grew. They were unlocking the secrets of an ancient civilization, and in doing so, they were laying the foundations for the future of humanity on Mars. The abandoned facilities, once silent and forgotten, were now bustling with activity, a testament to the pioneering spirit of the settlers and the enduring legacy of the Anunnaki.

The integration of Anunnaki technology with human ingenuity allowed the settlers to rapidly develop the colony. The energy systems and life support mechanisms left behind by the Anunnaki were harnessed and adapted to human needs, transforming what were once ancient relics into vital components of the new Martian infrastructure. The settlers used advanced Anunnaki solar collectors and energy storage units to create a robust power grid that could withstand the harsh conditions of the Martian environment. These systems provided a reliable and sustainable source of energy, allowing the colony to operate efficiently and continuously.

Greenhouses were established using advanced hydroponics, ensuring a steady food supply. The settlers constructed large, domed greenhouses, their transparent panels glinting under the Martian sun. Inside, rows of vibrant green plants thrived in nutrient-rich water, their growth accelerated by precise control of light, temperature, and humidity. This innovative agricultural setup not only provided fresh food but also produced oxygen and helped recycle water, creating a self-sustaining ecosystem. The sight of lush, green crops growing on the red planet was a symbol of hope and resilience, showcasing humanity's ability to adapt and flourish even in the most challenging environments.

The colony quickly transformed from a series of temporary shelters to a thriving hub of activity and innovation. The makeshift habitats gave way to permanent structures, built using materials synthesized from Martian soil combined with Anunnaki construction techniques. These buildings were equipped with advanced insulation and life support systems, providing comfortable living and working conditions for the settlers. Laboratories and workshops buzzed with activity as scientists and engineers worked on projects that ranged from medical research to environmental management.

One morning, as the settlers gathered in the central plaza for a community meeting, Musk addressed them with a sense of profound accomplishment. The central plaza, surrounded by the colony's most important buildings, had become the heart of the community. The settlers, clad in their work suits, looked up at Musk with expressions of pride and anticipation.

"We've come a long way from our first landing. Thanks to our hard work and the invaluable assistance from the Anunnaki, we are not just surviving on Mars; we are thriving," Musk announced, his voice filled with emotion. The settlers cheered, their spirits lifted by the recognition of their collective effort.

Dr. Zhang stepped forward, adding to Musk's sentiments. "The data we've collected from the Anunnaki facilities has opened up new avenues of research and development. We're on the brink of breakthroughs that could revolutionize life on Mars and beyond." Her words ignited a spark of excitement among the settlers. The knowledge they were uncovering had the potential to change the course of human history, not just on Mars but back on Earth and throughout the solar system.

As the settlers cheered, the sense of unity and purpose was undeniable. The challenges they had faced and overcome had forged a strong, resilient community. The colony was now a beacon of hope and progress, symbolizing humanity's ability to adapt, innovate, and reach for the stars. Each success, each innovation, was a testament to their hard work and the collaborative spirit fostered by their partnership with the Anunnaki.

In a quiet moment after the meeting, Musk stood with Dr. Zhang, looking out over the bustling colony. The settlement was alive with activity; settlers moved about, engaged in various tasks, while the hum of machinery and the chatter of conversations filled the air. "This is just the beginning, Sarah," he said quietly, his voice tinged with awe and determination. "Imagine what we can achieve in the years to come."

Dr. Zhang nodded, her eyes reflecting the same determination and optimism. "The possibilities are endless, Elon. With the knowledge we've gained here, there's no limit to what humanity can accomplish." They stood in silence for a moment, contemplating the future they were building.

As the sun set on the Martian horizon, casting long shadows over the colony, the settlers continued their work, driven by the shared dream of building a new world. The orange and red hues of the sunset painted the sky, creating a breathtaking backdrop for the burgeoning colony. The partnership with the Anunnaki had unlocked doors to a future that was once beyond imagination, and together, they were stepping boldly through those doors, ready to shape the destiny of humanity among the stars. The scene was a perfect blend of human perseverance and alien wisdom, heralding a new era of exploration and discovery.

CHAPTER 13: INANNA'S INFLUENCE

Inanna, with her unparalleled beauty and wisdom, became a cultural icon. Her presence was magnetic, drawing people from all walks of life. Politicians, scholars, artists, and ordinary citizens alike were captivated by her aura, and her influence extended far beyond diplomacy, inspiring a new wave of art, literature, and philosophy. Inanna's interactions with humans were always thoughtful and profound, leaving a lasting impression on everyone she met. Her words carried weight, and her ideas sparked a renaissance of creativity and intellectual exploration that reverberated across the globe.

One afternoon, Inanna attended an international art exhibition in Paris. The grand hall, resplendent with light filtering through stained glass windows, was filled with vibrant paintings, intricate sculptures, and innovative installations. The air buzzed with excitement as artists from around the world had come to showcase their work, many of them inspired by the new era of human-Anunnaki cooperation. The exhibition was a celebration of unity and the boundless possibilities of cross-cultural exchange.

As Inanna moved gracefully through the exhibits, her presence commanded attention. Her elegant attire and serene demeanor contrasted with the bustling energy around her. She paused in front of a large canvas depicting a futuristic cityscape where humans and Anunnaki lived in harmony. The painting was a breathtaking vision of a utopian future, with sleek architecture, lush green spaces, and vibrant communities working together.

The artist, a young woman named Aisha, approached nervously. Her heart raced as she neared Inanna, the figure who had inspired her most recent work. "Lady Inanna," Aisha began, her voice trembling slightly with a mix of awe and excitement, "it's an honor to have you here. This piece was inspired by your vision of unity and peace."

Inanna smiled warmly, her eyes reflecting genuine interest and kindness. She took a moment to study the painting closely, appreciating the intricate details and the vibrant colors that brought the scene to life. "It's beautiful, Aisha," Inanna said, her voice soft yet resonant. "Your art captures the essence of our shared future. It's through creations like this that we can inspire others to imagine and build a better world."

Her words resonated deeply with Aisha, who felt an overwhelming sense of validation and encouragement. She had poured her heart and soul into the piece, and Inanna's approval was the highest praise she could imagine. Tears of joy welled up in her eyes as she thanked Inanna. "Thank you, Lady Inanna. Your vision and wisdom have given us all so much hope."

This encounter was just one of many where Inanna's presence sparked a creative renaissance, rekindling humanity's creative spirit and leading to a flourishing of new ideas and expressions. Throughout the exhibition, other artists and attendees were inspired by her engagement and insights. She conversed with sculptors about the symbolism in their works, discussed with poets the themes of their verses, and encouraged musicians to explore new melodies that bridged cultural divides.

Inanna's influence permeated the event, creating an atmosphere of intellectual and artistic vigor. The conversations she sparked and the ideas she nurtured began to spread, fueling a broader cultural movement. Galleries, theaters, and concert halls around the world soon echoed with the newfound enthusiasm, showcasing works that celebrated the unity and potential of human and Anunnaki collaboration.

In the weeks and months following the exhibition, a surge of creative output emerged across various media. Writers penned novels and essays exploring the philosophical implications of a united interstellar community. Filmmakers produced documentaries and science fiction films inspired by Inanna's vision. Philosophers debated the ethical and existential questions posed by the blending of human and Anunnaki cultures.

Inanna's influence extended to academic institutions as well. Universities and research centers launched interdisciplinary programs to study the cultural, technological, and philosophical intersections of the two civilizations. Scholars and students alike were motivated to explore new fields of inquiry, driven by the same sense of wonder and possibility that Inanna had kindled.

Her impact was profound and far-reaching, touching every aspect of human endeavor. The creative renaissance she inspired was not just about producing art and literature; it was about fostering a new way of thinking, a new approach to solving problems, and a new appreciation for the diversity and interconnectedness of life. Inanna's legacy became a beacon of hope and a testament to the power of wisdom, beauty, and compassion in shaping a better future.

Men who interacted with Inanna were immediately mesmerized by her beauty and intellect. Her wisdom and grace were evident in every conversation, making her a captivating figure. Her presence exuded an aura of serenity and strength, drawing people to her effortlessly. Powerful leaders, drawn to her presence, often found themselves trying to impress and attract her, but Inanna was selective in her engagements. She valued intellect and compassion above all else, and her interactions reflected these values.

At a global summit in New York, world leaders gathered to discuss the future of interplanetary cooperation. The atmosphere was charged with anticipation, as discussions spanned topics from technological advancements to environmental sustainability. Among the attendees was Richard Blake, a wealthy industrialist known for his aggressive business tactics and inflated ego. Blake, always seeking to expand his influence, saw Inanna as an opportunity to further his ambitions.

During a break in the discussions, Blake approached Inanna with a confident swagger, his eyes gleaming with determination. "Lady Inanna," Blake said, bowing slightly in a gesture meant to impress, "I've heard so much about you. Perhaps we could discuss some of my innovative ideas for expanding our trade with the Anunnaki."

Inanna regarded him with a polite but distant smile, her eyes cool and assessing. "Mr. Blake, I appreciate your enthusiasm. However, true innovation comes from a place of genuine care and understanding, not just profit. Let's focus on how we can create a sustainable future for all."

Blake's confident demeanor faltered under her discerning gaze. Her words cut through his facade, revealing the shallowness of his intentions. "Of course, Lady Inanna," he stammered, clearly taken aback by her lack of interest in his proposals. "I'll, uh, think on that."

Inanna's response was firm but kind, reflecting her commitment to principles of empathy and integrity. She had no patience for those driven purely by self-interest, and her interactions with such individuals were brief and to the point.

In contrast, Inanna showed a keen interest in those who demonstrated intellect and compassion. Later that evening, she engaged in a deep conversation with Dr. Miguel Ramirez, a renowned environmental scientist dedicated to combating climate change. Dr. Ramirez had spent his career developing innovative solutions to preserve and restore the planet's ecosystems, and his passion for the environment resonated with

Inanna.

"Lady Inanna," Dr. Ramirez began, his voice filled with earnest curiosity, "I'm fascinated by Anunnaki environmental technologies. Could you share more about how your people achieve such harmony with nature?"

Inanna's eyes lit up with genuine enthusiasm, a radiant smile spreading across her face. "Dr. Ramirez, I would be delighted. Our technology is based on the principle of balance and respect for all life forms. It's about understanding the interconnectedness of our ecosystems and ensuring that every action we take benefits the whole."

Their conversation flowed effortlessly, filled with mutual respect and shared passion. Inanna explained how the Anunnaki harnessed renewable energy sources, implemented closed-loop agricultural systems, and developed advanced methods of waste management to maintain ecological balance. Dr. Ramirez listened intently, his mind racing with possibilities for applying these principles on Earth.

As they spoke, it became clear that Inanna valued individuals who sought to make a meaningful difference, rather than those driven by self-interest. Her interactions with Dr. Ramirez and others like him were marked by a deep sense of connection and mutual understanding. She encouraged and inspired them, not just with her words, but with the genuine warmth and wisdom she imparted.

Inanna's influence extended far beyond her immediate interactions. Her presence at the summit and the conversations she sparked led to a renewed focus on ethical leadership and sustainable innovation. Leaders and thinkers who had once been preoccupied with personal gain began to see the value in collaboration and long-term thinking.

Inanna's ability to discern true intent and foster genuine connections set a powerful example for others. Her impact was profound, guiding humanity towards a more compassionate and enlightened approach to progress. The men and women who interacted with her left changed, carrying forward the ideals she championed in their own work and lives.

Inanna's influence sparked a renaissance of thought and expression across the globe. Artists, writers, and philosophers drew inspiration from her wisdom and vision, leading to a resurgence of creative endeavors that transcended traditional boundaries. Her interactions with humans, whether through public appearances or personal conversations, left a profound impact, catalyzing a wave of intellectual and artistic innovation.

In a bustling café in Rome, a group of young philosophers gathered to discuss the implications of human-Anunnaki relations on their understanding of existence. The atmosphere was charged with excitement and curiosity, the air filled with the rich aroma of freshly brewed espresso and the hum of animated conversation. Luca, a passionate young thinker with an insatiable curiosity, led the discussion. His eyes bright with excitement, he addressed the group.

"Inanna speaks of balance and respect," Luca said, his voice resonating with conviction. "Her philosophy challenges us to rethink our relationship with the Earth and each other. It's a call to elevate our consciousness and transcend our current limitations."

Maria, an aspiring poet, nodded in agreement, her fingers absently tracing patterns on the table. "Her presence inspires me to write about unity and the beauty of diverse perspectives," she added, her voice soft yet fervent. "It's like we're on the cusp of a new age of enlightenment, where we can truly appreciate the interconnectedness of all life."

Their conversation continued late into the night, the café's dim lights casting a warm glow on their faces. Ideas and inspirations flowed freely, fueled by the profound teachings of Inanna. They debated the nature of existence, the potential for human-Anunnaki collaboration, and the ethical implications of their newfound knowledge. This intellectual fervor was mirrored in countless other gatherings around the world, as people explored new ways of thinking and expressing themselves.

One evening, during a cultural event in Kyoto, Inanna addressed a gathering of artists and intellectuals. The venue, a traditional Japanese hall with sliding paper doors and a serene garden outside, was filled with people eager to hear her speak. Her presence commanded attention, and as she began to speak, a hush fell over the audience.

"Humanity has always had a deep well of creativity and wisdom," she said, her voice serene and powerful. "Now, with our combined knowledge and experiences, we can create a future that reflects the best of us all. Let us embrace this renaissance and let it guide us towards a brighter tomorrow."

The audience erupted in applause, moved by her words and the vision she presented. Inanna's influence had ignited a global movement, a renaissance that celebrated the fusion of human and Anunnaki cultures. The arts flourished, with painters, sculptors, musicians, and writers all finding new inspiration in the ideas of unity and shared progress. Philosophical and scientific exploration also surged, with scholars delving into the new possibilities opened up by Anunnaki knowledge.

As the event concluded, Inanna stood with several prominent artists and thinkers, discussing their latest works and ideas. The exchange of knowledge and inspiration was palpable, a testament to the profound impact she had made. She listened intently, her eyes shining with interest and appreciation, offering insights and encouragement that further fueled their creative fires.

Inanna's presence on Earth was a beacon of wisdom and beauty, guiding humanity towards a new era of creativity and enlightenment. Her influence extended far beyond diplomacy, touching the very soul of human culture and rekindling the creative spirit that had always been at the heart of human progress. She became a symbol of the potential that lay within all beings to create, innovate, and transcend. Her legacy was not just one of technological advancement, but of a deeper understanding and appreciation for the shared journey of all sentient life.

Inanna, with her unparalleled beauty and wisdom, stood in the observation room, her eyes fixed on a monitor in the background where Jordan Peterson was giving a speech on compassion. The room was dimly lit, the soft hum of the monitor the only sound. She had intended to focus on her tasks, but Peterson's words, delivered with his characteristic intensity and eloquence, began to resonate deeply within her.

Peterson, speaking to a packed auditorium, addressed the fundamental human need for compassion. "Compassion," he began, his voice steady and clear, "is not just an emotion; it's a moral imperative. It's the recognition of another's suffering and the commitment to alleviate it, even at a cost to oneself."

Inanna tried to stay focused on her work, but Peterson's words cut through her concentration. His discourse on the profound importance of empathy, interwoven with stories of human struggle and resilience, struck a chord with her. She admired his intellect and the way he articulated complex truths with such clarity and passion.

Peterson continued, his voice growing more emotional. "We must strive to be compassionate, not because it's easy, but because it's necessary. Compassion is what binds us together as human beings, what allows us to overcome our greatest challenges and to find meaning in our lives."

Inanna felt a swell of emotion rising within her. She was a respected warrior, known for her strength and resilience, but Peterson's words touched something deep inside her. She had seen much in her long life, but the raw, unfiltered emotion in Peterson's voice brought tears to her eyes.

As Peterson began to break down, his voice trembling with the weight of his words, he said, "In a world so often filled with pain and suffering, compassion is the light that guides us through the darkness. It is the highest form of human expression, the essence of what it means to truly live."

Inanna, hiding her emotions as best she could, kept listening. The room seemed to close in around her, and her vision blurred with the tears she fought to hold back. The depth of Peterson's understanding, his ability to touch the soul of humanity, moved her profoundly. A single tear drop formed in her eye and slowly traced its way down her cheek.

Unable to contain her emotions any longer, Inanna excused herself. She turned away from the monitor, her steps light but purposeful as she left the room. She sought solitude, a place where she could gather her thoughts and process the intense feelings that Peterson's speech had stirred within her.

Despite her warrior's heart, Inanna had exceptional respect for Peterson's mind. His insights into the human condition, his unyielding quest for truth, and his unwavering compassion were qualities she held in the highest regard. In that moment, she felt a deep connection to his words, a reminder of the profound beauty and complexity of the human spirit.

Alone in the quiet of her private quarters, Inanna let her tears flow freely. She was moved not by sorrow, but by a profound sense of hope and admiration. Peterson's speech had reminded her of the strength that lies in vulnerability, the power of compassion to heal and transform. It was a lesson she would carry with her, a beacon of light in her ongoing journey.

CHAPTER 14: UNCOVERING THE PAST

Archaeological expeditions, guided by Anunnaki knowledge, embarked on a global quest to uncover more about Earth's ancient history. The Anunnaki, with their vast reservoirs of historical and technological wisdom, provided invaluable guidance, leading the teams to previously unknown sites. These locations, scattered across the globe, held secrets that had been buried for millennia, waiting to be revealed to the world once more.

In the dense jungles of South America, an expedition led by Dr. Anna Lopez made a groundbreaking discovery. The air was thick with humidity and the sounds of wildlife, the dense canopy overhead casting dappled shadows on the forest floor. Following ancient maps provided by Enki, the team unearthed a massive underground complex hidden beneath the lush vegetation. The entrance, covered by centuries of overgrowth and roots, was finally revealed after days of meticulous excavation, leading to a network of tunnels and chambers that seemed to extend endlessly into the earth.

As they ventured deeper, the team encountered advanced Anunnaki technology, preserved in remarkable condition despite the passage of time. The walls of the tunnels were smooth and cool to the touch, embedded with glowing symbols and holographic interfaces that flickered to life as they passed.

Dr. Lopez marveled at the intricate machinery, which seemed to hum with latent energy. "This technology is far beyond anything we have today," she remarked, her voice filled with awe and reverence. "Even though it's ancient, it still operates with a level of sophistication we can't yet fully comprehend."

The discovery included a variety of artefacts, from communication devices resembling crystal tablets that projected images and sounds, to what appeared to be advanced medical equipment capable of scanning and repairing biological tissues. The team also found small, handheld devices that seemed to be tools or instruments, their functions not immediately clear but suggestive of highly specialized uses.

The team's excitement grew with each new find, knowing they were uncovering a vital chapter of human history. Each artefact was carefully documented and analyzed, revealing new insights into the daily lives and technological prowess of the Anunnaki. They discovered detailed records etched into crystalline slabs, which depicted scenes of Anunnaki and humans interacting, sharing knowledge, and building together. These records provided a vivid narrative of cooperation and mutual respect that had once existed between the two species.

Dr. Lopez and her team felt a profound connection to the ancient beings who had once walked the same paths they now explored. The advanced medical equipment, for instance, hinted at a deep understanding of biology and healing that surpassed current human knowledge. One of the most striking finds was a chamber filled with what appeared to be educational tools, including interactive holographic displays that demonstrated complex scientific concepts in a visual and intuitive manner.

"This changes everything," Dr. Lopez said during a team meeting, her voice charged with enthusiasm. "We're not just finding artefacts; we're uncovering a lost civilization that had a profound impact on our own development. These discoveries will revolutionize our understanding of history and technology."

The expedition's progress was closely monitored and supported by Anunnaki experts who provided context and explanations for many of the findings. Enki himself visited the site, his presence lending further significance to the discoveries. "These technologies and records are a testament to the heights we reached and the knowledge we sought to share with humanity," he said, his voice resonating with pride and nostalgia.

The dense jungle of South America, once a silent guardian of ancient secrets, had become the stage for a historic revelation. The underground complex, with its preserved technology and artefacts, was a treasure trove of knowledge that promised to bridge the gap between past and present. As the expedition continued, the team knew that they were not just excavating physical remnants but also piecing together a narrative that connected the origins of human civilization with the guiding hand of the Anunnaki. The excitement and anticipation of what lay ahead were palpable, fueling their determination to uncover every hidden detail and unlock the full story of humanity's ancient allies.

The discoveries were not limited to functional technology. The expeditions also found what could only be described as Anunnaki toys and educational tools. These artefacts provided a unique glimpse into the daily lives of the Anunnaki and their interactions with early humans, revealing a culture that valued learning and development from a very young age.

In the sands of the Middle East, Dr. Samir Khalid's team uncovered a cache of small, intricately designed objects in a buried chamber near an ancient temple site. The sun beat down mercilessly as the archaeologists meticulously brushed away layers of sand to reveal these hidden treasures. The chamber's walls were adorned with faded frescoes depicting scenes of Anunnaki life, further adding to the richness of the discovery.

One of the most fascinating finds was a set of small, holographic projectors that, when activated, displayed three-dimensional images of stars, planets, and complex scientific concepts. The projectors, though ancient, still functioned perfectly, casting vivid and detailed holograms into the dusty air of the chamber. "These must have been used to educate young Anunnaki," Dr. Khalid speculated, holding one of the projectors delicately in his gloved hands. The device was made of a smooth, unknown material that felt warm to the touch. "It's incredible to think that even their toys were designed to teach and inspire."

The holograms were more than just static images; they were interactive, allowing users to manipulate the stars and planets with simple gestures. This level of interactivity suggested a highly sophisticated understanding of both technology and pedagogy. As Dr. Khalid demonstrated one of the projectors to his team, the room was filled with gasps of amazement. The projections included detailed explanations in an ancient script, possibly meant to guide young learners through the complexities of the universe.

The team also found interactive devices that seemed to be ancient games, designed not only for entertainment but also to enhance cognitive abilities and strategic thinking. These devices were small, portable, and intricately crafted, featuring movable parts and holographic displays. One game, in particular, involved solving complex puzzles that required a deep understanding of geometry and logic. "These are like nothing we've ever seen," one of the archaeologists remarked, marveling at the ingenuity of the design. "They show just how advanced the Anunnaki were in every aspect of their society."

The games and educational tools provided a window into the Anunnaki approach to learning and development. They suggested a society that placed immense value on intellectual growth and critical thinking. The artefacts indicated that the Anunnaki children were taught to think strategically and solve problems from an early age, skills that would have been crucial in a technologically advanced civilization.

In addition to the projectors and games, the team uncovered a variety of other educational artefacts, including what appeared to be instructional scrolls and manuals. These scrolls, written in the elegant Anunnaki script, detailed lessons in various subjects such as astronomy, mathematics, and engineering. The content was far more advanced than anything known from ancient human civilizations, indicating that the Anunnaki had a highly structured and comprehensive educational system.

Dr. Khalid and his team were struck by the sophistication and foresight of the Anunnaki. "These findings are not just relics of a bygone era," he said during a team meeting. "They are lessons for us today. They show us the importance of integrating education and play, and how early learning can shape a society's future."

The discoveries in the Middle East, much like those in other parts of the world, were not just about uncovering the past but also about understanding the principles that guided the Anunnaki. Their approach to education and development was holistic, combining practical skills with intellectual and emotional growth. This philosophy was evident in every artefact, from the simplest toy to the most complex educational tool.

The revelations from these archaeological expeditions provided a new perspective on the Anunnaki and their profound influence on early human civilizations. They painted a picture of a society that was not only technologically advanced but also deeply invested in the intellectual and moral development of its members. The artefacts were more than just historical curiosities; they were a testament to the enduring legacy of the Anunnaki and their commitment to nurturing knowledge and wisdom in all its forms.

As the expeditions continued, the teams uncovered artefacts that shed light on the origins of human civilization and the long-forgotten interactions with the Anunnaki. The discovery sites were spread across various terrains, each offering a unique glimpse into the intertwined history of the two species. In a remote desert region, a collaborative team of Anunnaki and human archaeologists discovered a site that contained detailed records of early human development. The dry, arid landscape concealed an ancient treasure trove beneath its sands, one that had remained hidden for millennia.

These records were inscribed on large, crystalline tablets that glowed with an inner light, a testament to the advanced technology of the Anunnaki. Each tablet was a masterpiece of craftsmanship, with inscriptions that seemed to pulse with a soft luminescence, making the ancient texts legible even in the dim light of the desert evening. The tablets were arranged in a circular formation, indicating their significance and the care with which they had been preserved.

Dr. Emily Hayes, who had initially discovered Nibiru, joined this expedition, feeling a profound connection to the ongoing revelations. Her hands trembled slightly as she held one of the crystalline tablets, the weight of history pressing down on her. As she studied the intricate symbols and diagrams, she realized they contained detailed accounts of genetic modifications and cultural exchanges. The inscriptions were written in a complex script that combined visual elements and linguistic symbols, requiring both Anunnaki and human scholars to decode.

"These records confirm that the Anunnaki played a significant role in shaping early human society," she said, her voice tinged with wonder. "They weren't just observers; they were active participants in our development." The tablets described how the Anunnaki had introduced advanced agricultural techniques, built monumental structures, and shared knowledge of astronomy and medicine. They had also conducted genetic experiments that enhanced human abilities and resilience, laying the foundation for civilization to flourish.

The artefacts also included artistic representations of Anunnaki and humans working together, building structures, and sharing knowledge. These images were etched into the crystalline tablets with exquisite detail, depicting scenes of harmonious coexistence. Anunnaki engineers and human builders were shown collaborating on massive architectural projects, while scholars from both species exchanged scrolls and diagrams in ancient academies.

One particularly striking tablet depicted a grand ceremonial event where Anunnaki and humans stood side by side, celebrating their shared achievements. The art conveyed a sense of unity and mutual respect, suggesting that the early relationship between the two species was one of collaboration rather than domination. The visual narrative was clear: humanity's early advancements were inextricably linked to the guidance and support of the Anunnaki.

One evening, as the team gathered around a campfire, Enki shared stories of those ancient times. The flickering flames cast shadows on the desert sand, creating an almost mystical atmosphere. "We saw potential in humanity," he said, his voice reflective. "Our goal was never to dominate, but to help you realize your potential. These discoveries are a testament to that shared journey." Enki's words resonated deeply with the team, reinforcing the sense of kinship and shared destiny that had grown between the Anunnaki and humans.

The discoveries made by these expeditions not only expanded the understanding of Earth's ancient history but also deepened the connection between humans and the Anunnaki. The artefacts and knowledge uncovered served as a bridge between the past and the present, illuminating the shared heritage and the long-forgotten interactions that had shaped the course of human civilization. Each artefact was a piece of a larger puzzle, revealing the complexities and depth of the Anunnaki's influence on human development.

As the teams continued their work, they felt a renewed sense of purpose. The ancient sites and technologies they uncovered were not just remnants of a distant past but also beacons guiding humanity towards a future of greater understanding and cooperation. The journey to uncover the past had just begun, and with each new discovery, the bond between humans and the Anunnaki grew stronger, paving the way for a future where the lessons of history would guide the path forward.

The artefacts provided invaluable insights into the technological advancements, cultural practices, and philosophical teachings of the Anunnaki. The tablets included detailed star maps, revealing the extent of Anunnaki exploration and their interactions with other civilizations. There were also records of environmental stewardship practices that could offer solutions to contemporary ecological challenges. The artefacts were meticulously cataloged and analyzed, with findings disseminated to academic institutions and research centers worldwide.

The collaborative efforts of the archaeologists, scientists, and historians involved in these expeditions fostered a sense of global unity. The shared goal of uncovering and understanding the Anunnaki's legacy transcended national and cultural boundaries, uniting people in a quest for knowledge and enlightenment. The bond between humans and the Anunnaki, strengthened by these joint ventures, promised a future where the wisdom of the past would illuminate the path to a harmonious and prosperous future for both species.

CHAPTER 15: UNITY AND PROGRESS

The world grew closer, united by the shared experience of the Anunnaki presence. The extraordinary revelations and technological advancements brought by the Anunnaki had a profound impact on global society. National borders became less relevant as humanity worked together towards common goals. The drive to explore the cosmos, improve quality of life, and preserve the planet's resources fostered unprecedented international cooperation. The sense of a shared destiny transcended previous geopolitical tensions, uniting diverse cultures and nations in a collective mission.

Governments formed new alliances, and global initiatives were launched to address pressing issues such as climate change, poverty, and disease. These efforts were coordinated through newly established international organizations that facilitated cooperation and resource-sharing on an unprecedented scale. Advanced Anunnaki technologies were applied to mitigate environmental damage, harness clean energy, and improve agricultural yields, providing sustainable solutions to some of the world's most intractable problems.

The collective efforts were not limited to political and economic spheres; they also encompassed cultural exchanges and joint scientific endeavors. People from different corners of the globe engaged in cultural programs that celebrated diversity while emphasizing common human values. Art, music, literature, and other forms of cultural expression flourished as artists drew inspiration from both human and Anunnaki influences. These exchanges enriched the global cultural landscape and fostered a deeper understanding and appreciation of different traditions.

Education and science flourished as resources were pooled and shared across borders, resulting in a renaissance of intellectual and technological advancement. International research collaborations became the norm, with scientists and engineers working together on projects that ranged from space exploration to medical research. The open exchange of knowledge accelerated innovation and led to breakthroughs that benefited all of humanity.

In this new era of unity, educational institutions played a pivotal role. Universities and research centers around the world became hubs of innovation and collaboration. These institutions expanded their curricula to include Anunnaki science and philosophy, preparing students to navigate and contribute to a rapidly changing world. Students from diverse backgrounds and nations studied together, exchanging ideas and working on groundbreaking projects. They were no longer just citizens of their respective countries but members of a global community with a shared future.

The spirit of cooperation and shared purpose permeated every aspect of society, leading to rapid progress and a sense of global community. Conferences, symposiums, and workshops brought together experts and enthusiasts from various fields to discuss and develop solutions to global challenges. The media, too, played a crucial role in disseminating information and fostering a sense of unity, highlighting stories of collaboration and innovation.

In this interconnected world, barriers to communication and collaboration were dismantled. Advances in translation technologies, influenced by Anunnaki linguistics, made it easier for people to share ideas and knowledge across language barriers. Virtual reality platforms enabled immersive cross-cultural experiences, allowing people to learn about and appreciate different cultures firsthand.

The impact of the Anunnaki presence was felt in everyday life as well. Communities around the world embraced new technologies that improved living standards and quality of life. Smart cities, powered by Anunnaki energy solutions, became models of efficiency and sustainability. Healthcare systems integrated Anunnaki medical advancements, providing more effective treatments and extending life expectancy.

The global community, united by the shared experience of the Anunnaki presence, was characterized by a renewed sense of hope and possibility. The challenges of the past seemed surmountable in the face of unprecedented cooperation and innovation. Humanity stood on the brink of a new era, one defined by a collective effort to explore the cosmos, improve quality of life, and ensure the sustainability of the planet for future generations. The legacy of the Anunnaki was not just their technology and knowledge, but the inspiration they provided for humanity to come together and achieve greatness.

At Swansea University, this spirit of collaboration was embodied by the partnership between Dr. Ken Griffin, a renowned Egyptology professor, and Graham Hancock, a celebrated researcher of ancient civilizations. The sheer vastness of discoveries being rediscovered necessitated their combined expertise. The university, already a center of excellence in archaeological research, became the focal point of their efforts to unravel the mysteries of ancient Egypt in the context of Anunnaki influence.

Dr. Griffin was called upon for his deep knowledge of Egyptology. His understanding of hieroglyphics, ancient Egyptian culture, and archaeology was invaluable in interpreting the new findings. With his extensive experience in deciphering ancient texts and symbols, Dr. Griffin meticulously analyzed inscriptions that had long puzzled historians. His ability to contextualize these discoveries within the broader narrative of Egyptian history provided a solid foundation for their research.

Graham Hancock, with his extensive experience in exploring ancient mysteries and connecting the dots between disparate historical events, brought a unique perspective to their work. Hancock's unconventional approaches and theories often challenged established academic thought, making him the perfect complement to Griffin's more traditional expertise. His ability to synthesize information from various disciplines allowed him to see patterns and connections that others might overlook.

Together, they embarked on an ambitious project to re-examine the ancient sites and artefacts of Egypt through the lens of Anunnaki involvement. Their collaboration was marked by a rigorous yet open-minded approach, combining the best of academic scholarship with innovative thinking. This synergy was essential as they delved into the depths of Egypt's storied past, uncovering layers of history that had remained hidden for millennia.

Their research took them from the towering pyramids of Giza to the enigmatic ruins of Abydos. At Giza, they re-examined the Great Pyramid with a fresh perspective, considering it not just as a monumental tomb, but as a possible center of Anunnaki technology and knowledge. Detailed studies of the pyramid's construction techniques revealed signs of advanced engineering principles that aligned with Anunnaki technological prowess. Griffin's expertise in hieroglyphics helped decode new messages and symbols that pointed to a more intricate relationship between the pharaohs and the Anunnaki.

In Abydos, one of Egypt's oldest and most sacred sites, they discovered previously overlooked inscriptions and artefacts that hinted at a deeper connection between the Anunnaki and early Egyptian civilization. These findings included detailed carvings depicting celestial beings interacting with humans, sharing knowledge and technology. The intricate artwork suggested a level of sophistication and understanding far beyond what was previously believed to be within the capabilities of early Egyptians.

The inscriptions detailed accounts of visits from celestial beings who brought with them not only knowledge but also tools and technologies that helped shape the foundation of Egyptian society. Artefacts such as precisely cut stone tools and advanced medical instruments were found, their craftsmanship echoing the advanced technologies the Anunnaki were known for. Griffin and Hancock realized these artefacts were not merely symbolic but functional, revealing a practical aspect to the Anunnaki's influence.

Their discoveries were meticulously documented, with detailed photographs, translations, and analyses being shared with the global academic community. The collaboration at Swansea University attracted scholars and researchers from around the world, eager to contribute to and learn from this groundbreaking work. Lectures, symposiums, and publications stemming from their findings spurred a renewed interest in Egyptology and ancient civilizations, inspiring a new generation of researchers.

The partnership between Dr. Griffin and Graham Hancock at Swansea University exemplified the power of interdisciplinary collaboration. By combining their unique strengths, they were able to uncover a richer, more complex history of ancient Egypt, one that highlighted the profound impact of Anunnaki involvement. Their work not only advanced academic understanding but also captivated the public imagination, fostering a deeper appreciation for the interconnectedness of human history and the cosmos.

Dr. Griffin is an extreme expert in fieldwork; his entire life has been spent visiting Egypt and Sudan, harvesting great results and popularity for Swansea University. Known for his meticulous attention to detail and his ability to uncover hidden treasures, Griffin's reputation as a leading Egyptologist was well-earned. His deep commitment to unearthing the secrets of the ancient world made him a natural partner for Graham Hancock, whose innovative theories often required rigorous archaeological validation.

The partnership between Dr. Griffin and Hancock yielded remarkable discoveries. Their combined expertise allowed them to uncover insights that had eluded scholars for centuries. In the Valley of the Kings, an area renowned for its royal tombs, they made one of their most significant finds. After months of careful excavation, they uncovered a hidden chamber filled with artefacts that bore unmistakable signs of Anunnaki craftsmanship. The chamber, which had been sealed for millennia, was a treasure trove of ancient technology and historical records.

Among the items were intricately designed tools and devices, some of which appeared to be far more advanced than anything previously discovered from that era. The craftsmanship and materials used were unlike those of typical Egyptian artefacts, pointing clearly to an otherworldly origin. Tablets inscribed with detailed accounts of interactions between the Anunnaki and the pharaohs provided new insights into the technological and cultural exchanges that had shaped ancient Egypt. These records described how the Anunnaki shared knowledge of engineering, medicine, and astronomy, significantly advancing Egyptian society.

One of their most significant discoveries was a series of scrolls that chronicled the construction of the Great Pyramid. These scrolls were found in a sealed stone chest within the hidden chamber, perfectly preserved thanks to the dry, stable conditions. The scrolls revealed that the Anunnaki had provided crucial knowledge and assistance in its design and construction, using advanced techniques that had been lost to history. Detailed diagrams showed the use of anti-gravity devices to move massive stones and the application of precise mathematical principles that aligned the pyramid with celestial bodies.

The revelation reshaped the understanding of this iconic monument, highlighting the collaborative effort between humans and Anunnaki. The Great Pyramid, long considered a marvel of human engineering, was now seen as a symbol of interstellar cooperation. This new perspective sparked widespread interest and debate among historians, archaeologists, and the public.

Dr. Griffin and Hancock also unearthed a network of tunnels beneath the Sphinx, leading to a subterranean complex that contained a wealth of information about Anunnaki technology and their influence on human civilization. The tunnels were filled with artefacts, including advanced machinery, energy devices, and even what appeared to be a communication hub. These findings were meticulously documented and shared with the global scientific community, sparking further research and debate.

During a conference at Swansea University, Dr. Griffin addressed an audience of scholars and students, showcasing their discoveries. Standing before a packed auditorium, he presented detailed images and data from their expeditions. "These artefacts and records provide undeniable evidence of the Anunnaki's significant role in shaping ancient Egypt," he said, his voice echoing with excitement and authority. "Our work is just beginning, but it is clear that the Anunnaki were more than myth; they were integral to our history."

Hancock added, "The implications of these findings are profound. They challenge our understanding of history and open up new avenues of exploration. We must continue to work together, across disciplines and borders, to uncover the full story of our shared past." His words resonated with the audience, underscoring the importance of collaboration and the pursuit of knowledge.

As the world absorbed these revelations, the sense of unity and progress grew stronger. The collaborative efforts of Dr. Griffin, Hancock, and countless other researchers around the globe symbolized the potential of a united humanity. Their discoveries not only expanded the understanding of Earth's ancient history but also deepened the connection between humans and the Anunnaki, paving the way for a future where the lessons of history would guide the path forward.

The discoveries had a profound impact on educational curricula worldwide. Schools and universities integrated the new findings into their history and science programs, fostering a generation of students inspired by the unity of human and Anunnaki achievements. Museums created exhibits showcasing the artefacts, drawing visitors from around the world and further spreading the message of global collaboration.

The partnership between Dr. Griffin and Graham Hancock at Swansea University stood as a beacon of what could be achieved through cooperation and shared knowledge. Their work not only advanced the field of Egyptology but also demonstrated the power of unity in overcoming the mysteries of the past. As they continued their research, the world watched with bated breath, eager to see what other secrets the sands of Egypt might reveal.

CHAPTER 16: THE FINAL GOLD SHIPMENT

The day had finally arrived. The Anunnaki, having completed their mission on Earth, were preparing to depart. The final shipment of gold, meticulously extracted and refined, was ready to be transported back to Nibiru. This moment had been anticipated with a mixture of excitement and solemnity, as it marked the culmination of an extraordinary chapter in human history. Across the globe, people gathered in open spaces, city squares, parks, and fields, craning their necks skyward in silent anticipation as the Anunnaki ships began to appear on the horizon. The atmosphere was thick with awe and reverence, as the world collectively held its breath.

The sight was nothing short of awe-inspiring. The ships were colossal, their immense scale becoming apparent as they descended through the atmosphere with a grace that defied their size. Their gleaming hulls, crafted from a material unknown to humanity, reflected the sunlight in dazzling arrays of light, creating a spectacle of brilliance that filled the sky. The surface of each vessel appeared almost fluid, rippling like liquid silver as they moved, catching and scattering light in every direction. These ships, each a masterpiece of design, showcased the advanced engineering of the Anunnaki, blending aesthetic beauty with immense power.

As the ships approached Earth, the very air around them

seemed to shift and dance, reacting to the presence of these otherworldly vessels. The clouds, once drifting aimlessly across the sky, were drawn towards the ships, pulled into intricate spirals and vortexes as if the vessels themselves were orchestrating the movement of the skies. It was as though the ships commanded the elements, bending the atmosphere to their will. The clouds, now tinged with shades of gold and pink from the setting sun, wrapped around the ships in a delicate, almost tender embrace. The sky transformed into a canvas of surreal, otherworldly beauty, acelestial dance between light, color, and form that left onlookers mesmerized.

Below, the human vehicles, trucks, cranes, and specialized transport carriers, appeared minuscule in comparison. These vehicles, which had played a crucial role in transporting the final bars of gold to the departure sites, now seemed insignificant, almost like children's toys, when juxtaposed against the enormity of the Anunnaki ships. Even the largest of human-made machines, marvels of industrial engineering in their own right, looked diminutive and fragile next to these extraterrestrial behemoths. The contrast was stark and humbling, a visual reminder of the vast technological gap between the two civilizations. It was a humbling sight, one that underscored the profound difference in scale and capability between humanity and their ancient visitors.

The ships hovered with a serene, almost majestic stillness, their massive forms blotting out the sun in places, casting long, dark shadows over the land. Yet, there was no sense of foreboding, only awe and admiration. The vessels exuded a quiet power, a testament to the advanced technology and knowledge of the Anunnaki. The humans on the ground, dwarfed by the sheer size of the ships, could only look on in wonder, their hearts filled with a mix of gratitude and melancholy as they prepared to say farewell to the beings who had so profoundly impacted their world.

As more ships joined the fleet, the sky became a breathtaking panorama of motion and light, an extraordinary tapestry woven by the graceful movements of the Anunnaki vessels. Each ship, an immense structure of unimaginable complexity, moved with a fluidity that belied its colossal size. They glided through the air with an elegance that seemed almost magical, as if they were not bound by the same physical laws that governed earthly machines. The sheer scale of the ships was staggering, yet they maneuvered as if weightless, their presence in the sky both majestic and serene.

The arrival of each new vessel sent ripples through the atmosphere, like a stone dropped into a still pond. These ripples caused the clouds to part and reform in their wake, creating dynamic patterns that rippled outwards from the ships' paths. It was as though the very fabric of the sky was being reshaped by their passage, responding to their movement with a symphony of shifting shapes and colors. Some ships hovered low, their enormous hulls casting vast, sweeping shadows over the landscape below. These shadows moved slowly across the ground, like the passing of clouds, giving the earth a fleeting, twilight hue. Other ships remained higher in the sky, their outlines shimmering like silver ghosts against the deepening blue, as the day began to surrender to the approaching dusk.

On the ground, the teams of human workers moved with coordinated precision, their efforts dwarfed but not diminished by the scale of the task at hand. Cranes, powerful and advanced by human standards, lifted the heavy gold bars with an ease that belied their weight. The bars, each gleaming with a rich, golden hue, were carefully placed onto the open bays of the Anunnaki ships. These bays, vast and cavernous, were designed to hold enormous quantities of material, their interiors echoing with the sound of the precious cargo being secured. The ground teams, aware of the historic significance of this moment, worked with a diligence born of both respect and reverence.

As the last of the gold was secured, a deep, resonant hum began to emanate from the ships. This sound, barely perceptible at first, gradually grew in intensity, filling the air with a vibration that could be felt as much as heard. It was a sound that resonated within every being present, a low, calming frequency that seemed to reach into the very core of those who heard it. The hum was almost musical, a deep, otherworldly note that spoke of power, mystery, and the ancient knowledge of the Anunnaki. It was as if the ships themselves were communicating with the world around them, acknowledging the completion of their mission and preparing for their departure.

Above, the clouds continued their intricate dance around the ships, forming spirals and loops that seemed to defy the laws of physics. The vessels appeared to exert a subtle influence over the weather, drawing moisture from the atmosphere and creating a delicate mist that clung to their hulls. This mist, fine as gossamer, condensed around the ships, refracting the fading light of the sun into a spectrum of colors. Halos of rainbow hues formed around each vessel, the soft, iridescent light wrapping them in a celestial glow. It was as if the sky itself was celebrating this momentous occasion, offering a final, ethereal tribute to the departing Anunnaki.

The visual spectacle was mesmerizing, a blend of natural beauty and technological marvel that left the onlookers below in silent awe. The sight of the ships, encircled by these radiant halos, was otherworldly, a reminder of the cosmic forces at play in this historic moment. The world seemed to hold its breath, the air charged with a sense of both completion and anticipation. As the ships prepared to ascend, the sky, now a riot of colors and light, stood as a testament to the unprecedented collaboration between humans and the Anunnaki, a partnership that had reshaped the world and expanded the horizons of possibility.

The final preparations complete, the ships hovered momentarily, their vibrant halos shimmering in the twilight. The mist around them thickened slightly, catching the last rays of the setting sun and casting the landscape below in a golden, ethereal light. The earth and sky seemed united in a silent farewell, a mutual acknowledgment of the significance of this departure. The clouds, having played their part in this grand spectacle, slowly began to dissipate, leaving the ships bathed in the soft glow of dusk.

The stage was set for the Anunnaki's final ascent, the culmination of their time on Earth and the fulfillment of an ancient promise. The world watched, mesmerized, as the ships, now radiant beacons in the sky, prepared to embark on their journey home.

With the last of the gold secured, the Anunnaki ships began to ascend, their massive forms lifting gracefully from the earth. At first, their movement was slow and deliberate, as if savoring these final moments on the planet they had once called home. The hum of their engines, a deep and resonant sound, filled the air, growing louder and more powerful with each passing second. This hum was not just a noise; it was a vibration that could be felt deep within the earth, reverberating through the ground and up into the bodies of the onlookers, a physical reminder of the immense power contained within these otherworldly vessels.

The human vehicles below, which had played their part in loading the precious cargo, now appeared as tiny, insignificant dots beneath the ascending giants. The cranes and trucks, dwarfed to the point of near invisibility, began to retreat, moving back to a safe distance as the ships climbed higher into the sky. The golden bars, each meticulously refined and loaded, that had once been the pinnacle of human wealth, now seemed to fade into the background, becoming part of something far greater. They were no longer symbols of earthly riches but components of an interstellar mission, destined to journey far beyond the borders of Earth, contributing to the survival and prosperity of an ancient civilization on a distant world.

As the ships ascended, their speed gradually increased, and they began to cut through the clouds that had gathered around them. These clouds, once swirling and dancing around the vessels, now started to disperse, leaving behind delicate trails of mist that lingered momentarily in the ships' wake. The sun, hanging low on the horizon, cast long, golden beams of light through the dissipating clouds, catching the edges of the ships and illuminating them in a warm, radiant glow. The vessels, now bathed in this ethereal light, appeared almost otherworldly, glowing like celestial bodies ascending towards the heavens.

The sight was mesmerizing. The ships, with their golden halos, seemed to pierce through the very fabric of the sky, ascending steadily and purposefully through the remaining cloud cover. As they climbed higher, they left behind a sky that seemed suddenly vast and empty, devoid of the majestic forms that had so recently dominated it. The clouds, which had been drawn into intricate patterns by the ships' presence, slowly began to reform, returning to the more familiar shapes and movements dictated by the natural currents of the atmosphere.

On the ground, people watched in silent reverence, their eyes following the ships as they disappeared into the stratosphere. There was a collective stillness, a shared moment of awe and reflection, as the last of the Anunnaki vessels vanished from sight. The sky, now returning to its natural state, seemed to hold a sense of finality, yet also a promise of new beginnings. The departure of the Anunnaki marked the end of an era, a chapter in human history that had been both extraordinary and transformative. It was a moment that would be remembered for generations to come, a testament to the unprecedented collaboration between humans and an ancient extraterrestrial race.

This partnership had not only reshaped human society but had also left an indelible mark on the collective consciousness of the planet. The world had witnessed something truly extraordinary, an alliance that had bridged the gap between two vastly different civilizations, fostering a sense of unity and progress that would endure long after the ships had gone. The final gold shipment, now on its way to Nibiru, was more than just a physical exchange; it was a symbol of the possibilities that lay ahead, of a future where humanity might continue to reach for the stars.

As the last ship faded into the distance, a collective exhale seemed to ripple across the globe. It was a breath of relief, of closure, but also of anticipation. The weight of the moment was palpable, yet there was also a lightness, a feeling that the world had been forever changed, and that this change was just the beginning. The sky, now clear and expansive once more, seemed to whisper a promise to those who stood beneath it, a promise that this was not the end, but rather the beginning of a new journey for humanity. A journey that would take them further than they had ever imagined, guided by the lessons and legacy left behind by the Anunnaki. The future was vast and filled with possibilities, and humanity, united and inspired, was ready to embrace it.

CHAPTER 17: A NEW DAWN

As the final Anunnaki ship vanished into the depths of the stratosphere, the night sky above Earth transformed into a spectacle of celestial grandeur. The departure of these ancient travelers seemed to have awakened the cosmos itself. The stars, which had been mere pinpoints of light, now shimmered with an intensity that was almost otherworldly, as though they were alive and bearing witness to this historic moment. Their brilliance was so striking that it felt as if the stars were gazing back at Earth, their light imbued with the wisdom and knowledge of countless millennia.

The sky was a deep, velvety black, the kind of darkness that enveloped the world in a comforting embrace, allowing the stars to shine with unparalleled clarity. This was a darkness not of absence, but of depth, a canvas that stretched infinitely, drawing the gaze upwards into the mysteries of the universe. Against this backdrop, the stars appeared closer, more vivid, their light piercing the night with a crystalline sharpness. Constellations that had long guided human navigators now pulsed with renewed life, their familiar patterns glowing as if they were energized by the departure of the Anunnaki. It was as if these celestial formations, as ancient as the Anunnaki themselves, were sending a silent farewell to the visitors who had once walked among them.

The moon, a silent sentinel, hung low on the horizon, its presence both comforting and majestic. It cast a silver path across the oceans and deserts, a luminous bridge that connected the Earth to the heavens. This ethereal glow bathed the world in a soft, cool light, transforming the landscape into a dreamscape of silver and blue. The oceans, calm and expansive, mirrored the heavens above with a clarity that made it difficult to distinguish where the sky ended and the sea began. The reflection of the stars on the water created the illusion of a world suspended between two skies, as if Earth itself was floating in an endless cosmos, untethered and free. The horizon seemed to stretch infinitely, offering a glimpse into the boundless potential that lay ahead for humanity.

In cities and towns around the world, lights were dimmed in a collective act of reverence. People gathered on rooftops, in parks, and in open fields, their faces turned skyward in silent contemplation. The departure of the Anunnaki was not just a visual spectacle; it was a moment of profound significance that transcended words. The entire planet seemed to hold its breath, united in a shared sense of awe and wonder. This was not merely the end of a physical journey, but the culmination of an epoch in human history, one marked by discovery, cooperation, and the realization that humanity was not alone in the universe.

As the final trails of the ships' departure faded, dissolving into the vastness of space, the night sky remained untouched and endless, a reminder of the infinite possibilities that lay ahead. The world below stood united in awe, the silence punctuated only by the soft whispers of the wind. It was as if the universe itself had paused, acknowledging the significance of this transition,the end of an era and the beginning of a new chapter in human history. The departure of the Anunnaki had left an indelible mark on the collective consciousness of the planet, a reminder of the vastness of the cosmos and the potential within humanity to reach for the stars. In that moment, under the vast, starlit sky, the world felt both small and immense, as humanity prepared to take its next steps into the unknown, guided by the legacy of those who had come before

As the night gave way to dawn, the sky began its gentle

transformation, lightening slowly, as if the heavens themselves were stirring from a deep, contemplative rest. The darkness that had enveloped the world for hours began to retreat, giving way to a soft, diffused light that gradually filled the horizon. The transition from night to day was a symphony of colors, a gradual shift through a spectrum of hues that heralded the arrival of a new day. The deep blues and purples of the night were replaced by the first glimmers of dawn, a delicate pink that blushed across the sky, followed by the warm, golden tones that accompanied the rising sun. It was as if the Earth itself was awakening, shaking off the remnants of sleep and preparing to greet the new day with a renewed sense of purpose.

The first rays of the sun peeked over the horizon, tentative at first, casting a soft, golden light that gently caressed the landscape. This light, warm and nurturing, gradually grew in strength, washing away the last vestiges of night. The interplay of light and shadow created a sense of depth, as the long shadows cast by trees, buildings, and mountains slowly shortened, revealing the world in all its glory. The transition was almost magical, a quiet, yet profound moment where the world seemed to hold its breath, savoring the peacefulness of the dawn. The morning mist, which had settled over the land like a blanket during the night, began to lift, dissipating into the air as the sun's rays touched the earth. This mist, thin and ephemeral, hovered just above the ground, adding a dreamlike quality to the landscapes it covered.

As the mist lifted, the world below was gradually unveiled, each feature of the landscape touched by the first light of day. The clouds, still lingering from the night before, caught the sun's rays and were transformed into a canvas of gold and pink. Their edges, illuminated by the sun, glowed with a fiery brilliance that contrasted beautifully with the softer pastels of the sky. These clouds, once dark and mysterious, now floated like golden drifts, their shapes and forms shifting gently in the morning breeze. The sky itself, now a vast expanse of pastel hues, seemed to stretch infinitely, a reminder of the endless possibilities that lay ahead. It was as if the heavens were offering a silent blessing, encouraging the world to embrace the new day with hope and optimism.

The sun, still low in the sky, continued its steady ascent, casting long shadows across the ground. These shadows, deep and pronounced, created a play of light and dark that added depth and dimension to the world below. Every tree, every building, every mountain was highlighted in sharp relief, their forms standing out clearly against the backdrop of the sky. The light, rich and golden, bathed the Earth in warmth, as if to infuse the very ground with energy and life. The landscapes, from the towering peaks of distant mountains to the sprawling cities still waking from the night's slumber, were illuminated in crisp detail. The clarity of the morning light brought everything into focus, revealing the world in a way that felt both new and familiar.

As the sun rose higher, the full splendor of the morning was revealed. The Earth, now fully bathed in the warmth of the new day, seemed to pulse with life and energy. The shadows shortened, their edges softening, as the light became more direct and encompassing. The colors of the dawn deepened, becoming richer, more vibrant, as the sun climbed further into the sky. The day, still fresh and young, was filled with the promise of new beginnings, a clean slate on which anything was possible. The energy of the morning was palpable, a quiet yet powerful force that seemed to permeate everything, urging the world forward.

The skies, now clear and a brilliant shade of blue, stood as a backdrop to the dawn of a new era. The clarity of the sky, free of the clouds and mists of the night, symbolized the potential for humanity to chart its own course, unencumbered by the shadows of the past. The knowledge and technology left behind by the Anunnaki were now tools for the future, guiding humanity as they stepped into this new day. The world was ready to move forward, filled with the energy and optimism of a new beginning. As the sun continued to rise, its light spread across the land, touching every corner of the Earth, a reminder that the future was bright, and that humanity was poised to embrace it.

With the Anunnaki's departure, humanity faced the daunting yet exhilarating challenge of continuing the progress they had inspired. The departure of these ancient visitors marked the beginning of a new chapter in human history, one where the tools and knowledge left behind would serve as the foundation for an era of unparalleled exploration and discovery. The technologies bequeathed by the Anunnaki, though rooted in wisdom that spanned eons, were advanced beyond anything humanity had ever conceived. These were not merely relics of a bygone civilization; they were gifts, entrusted to the people of Earth to nurture and expand upon, fostering a future filled with promise and infinite potential.

One of the most significant technologies left behind was the Anunnaki's energy generation systems. These systems, based on principles of quantum resonance and zero-point energy, offered an inexhaustible source of power. The technology was both elegant and profound, harnessing the very fabric of the universe to generate clean, sustainable energy. Large crystalline structures, discovered deep within subterranean chambers, acted as conduits for this energy. These crystals, shimmering with an inner light, channeled the energy with incredible efficiency, their surfaces etched with intricate patterns that resonated with the frequencies of the quantum fields.

These crystalline structures were seamlessly integrated into Earth's energy grid, transforming the way power was distributed and consumed. The impact was immediate and profound. Cities that had once struggled with power shortages were now bathed in a constant, clean energy supply. The need for fossil fuels and other environmentally damaging energy sources became a thing of the past, as the world embraced this new, inexhaustible power. Even the most remote regions, which had been long cut off from modern amenities, now thrived, their communities powered by the silent hum of the crystalline energy grids. The transformation was nothing short of revolutionary, leading to an age of unprecedented innovation and growth. The newfound energy abundance spurred advancements in technology, infrastructure, and quality of life, as humanity entered a golden age of development.

Another groundbreaking technology was in the field of medicine. Anunnaki healing chambers, discovered in various hidden locations around the globe, contained advanced regenerative technology that could repair and rejuvenate human tissue at the cellular level. These chambers, with their soft, pulsating lights and soothing vibrations, were unlike anything humanity had ever encountered. The technology worked by stimulating the body's natural healing processes, using advanced nanotechnology and bio resonance frequencies to accelerate cell regeneration and repair damaged tissues. The chambers could cure diseases that had long plagued humanity, from chronic illnesses to previously incurable genetic conditions. They could even reverse the effects of aging, restoring vitality and extending life expectancy.

The integration of this technology into hospitals and medical centers revolutionized healthcare. Conditions that had once been considered terminal were now treatable, and patients who had lost hope found themselves given a second chance at life. The impact on society was profound, as people lived longer, healthier lives, free from the burden of disease and disability. The ripple effects of this advancement were felt across all sectors, from the workforce to the family unit, as individuals and communities thrived in ways previously thought impossible.

Transportation, too, was revolutionized. The anti-gravity propulsion systems, left behind in the Anunnaki's abandoned facilities, were adapted for human use, transforming the way people and goods moved across the planet, and beyond. Hovercraft and personal flying vehicles, once the stuff of science fiction, became commonplace. These vehicles, powered by silent anti-gravity engines, glided effortlessly over landscapes, leaving no trace of their passage. The environmental impact was negligible, as the vehicles produced no emissions, and their operation was entirely sustainable.

Long-distance travel was now measured in minutes rather than hours. What once took days by plane could now be accomplished in a fraction of the time, as human-built spacecraft, inspired by Anunnaki designs, began exploring not just the solar system, but the farthest reaches of the galaxy. The stars, which had once seemed so distant and unreachable, were now within humanity's grasp. The dream of interstellar travel was no longer a distant fantasy, but a reality, as humanity embarked on journeys to distant planets and unexplored regions of space. New frontiers were opened, and the spirit of exploration that had driven humanity for millennia was rekindled with a fervor not seen since the age of discovery.

The Anunnaki also left behind vast repositories of knowledge, libraries filled with data, holographic records, and interactive simulations that contained the accumulated wisdom of their civilization. These repositories were more than just archives; they were living monuments to the Anunnaki's legacy, designed to be explored, studied, and expanded upon. The data within these libraries covered every conceivable topic, from advanced scientific principles to the history of the cosmos, from philosophical treatises to detailed records of the Anunnaki's interactions with other civilizations across the galaxy.

These repositories were opened to the global community, and their contents were quickly integrated into educational systems around the world. Schools, universities, and research institutions became centers of learning and innovation, as students and scholars delved into the vast oceans of knowledge left behind by the Anunnaki. The impact on human culture was profound, as new ideas, philosophies, and technologies emerged from the study of these ancient records. Humanity's understanding of the universe expanded exponentially, as the knowledge of the Anunnaki was combined with human creativity and ingenuity.

CHAPTER 18: LEGACY OF THE ANUNNAKI

The legacy of the Anunnaki was felt in every corner of the globe, a pervasive influence that transformed human civilization in ways that would be felt for generations to come. Their arrival, marked by a deep exchange of knowledge and technology, had ignited a passion for progress that transcended borders and cultures. The Anunnaki had not only introduced advanced technologies that revolutionized industries, medicine, and transportation, but they had also imparted a sense of unity and purpose that had been lacking in human society.

In the years following their departure, the world found itself united in a shared mission to honor the gifts left behind by the Anunnaki. The once-divisive barriers between nations began to dissolve as humanity embraced the idea of a global community. Collaborative efforts between countries became the norm rather than the exception, and international projects were launched with unprecedented speed and success. The drive to explore the cosmos, to innovate, and to solve the challenges that had long plagued humanity was now fueled by the Anunnaki's vision of what was possible.

Education systems around the world were overhauled, integrating the vast repositories of Anunnaki knowledge into curricula. Students were no longer limited by the constraints of human history but were now learning from the experiences of a civilization that had explored the stars. This new generation, inspired by the Anunnaki's teachings, grew up with a deep-seated belief in the power of knowledge and the importance of collaboration. Universities and research centers flourished, becoming hubs of innovation where human creativity and Anunnaki wisdom combined to push the boundaries of what was possible.

Culturally, the impact of the Anunnaki was profound. Artists, writers, and thinkers found themselves inspired by the possibilities of the future, creating works that reflected the newfound sense of hope and unity. The themes of interconnectedness and the shared human destiny became central to artistic expression, resonating deeply with people around the world. The Anunnaki had left behind more than just technology, they had rekindled the creative spirit of humanity, encouraging exploration not just of the physical world, but of the realms of thought, imagination, and spirit.

The memory of the Anunnaki's visit served as a constant reminder of the potential for greatness within humanity. Monuments were erected in their honor, and museums dedicated to the history of the Anunnaki and their time on Earth became places of pilgrimage. These institutions were not just about preserving the past, but about inspiring the future. The Anunnaki had shown humanity what could be achieved when knowledge, compassion, and unity were placed at the forefront of civilization.

In every sphere of life, the influence of the Anunnaki was evident. From the clean, renewable energy that powered the world's cities, to the advanced medical treatments that had eradicated diseases, to the exploration of distant planets that was now a reality, the legacy of the Anunnaki was woven into the very fabric of human existence. It was a legacy of progress, of unity, and of a future that was brighter than ever before.

The world had changed, and it was for the better. The Anunnaki had come as visitors, but they left as mentors, their legacy a guiding light for humanity as it stepped confidently into a new era. The potential for greatness that they had seen in humanity was now being realized, as the people of Earth embraced their role as stewards of their planet and explorers of the stars. The journey was far from over, but with the Anunnaki's legacy as their foundation, humanity was ready to reach for the stars, united in purpose and driven by the belief that their greatest achievements were still to come.

Elon Musk's Mars colony, once a daring vision of the future, had now become a thriving reality. Nestled in the rugged, rust-colored terrain of the red planet, the colony, officially named New Horizons, stood as a testament to human ingenuity and determination. What had started as a modest settlement of scientists and engineers had rapidly expanded into a bustling hub of activity, innovation, and exploration. New Horizons was more than just a colony; it was a symbol of humanity's resilience and its unyielding desire to reach beyond the confines of Earth.

The colony thrived in ways that few had anticipated. Advanced agricultural domes, powered by Anunnaki technologies, produced abundant food, ensuring that the settlers were not only self-sufficient but also able to experiment with new forms of sustainable farming. These domes, with their transparent walls and ceilings, allowed the settlers to gaze up at the Martian sky while they worked, a constant reminder of the vastness of space and the endless possibilities that lay ahead.

New Horizons became a center of research and development, where human and Anunnaki technologies were further refined and adapted to the Martian environment. Laboratories buzzed with activity as scientists, both human and Anunnaki, worked side by side to unlock the secrets of the planet and explore new frontiers in science and engineering. The discoveries made in these labs, ranging from new propulsion systems to breakthroughs in material science, were not only critical for the survival and expansion of the Mars colony but also held the potential to revolutionize life on Earth.

The settlement's infrastructure, too, was a marvel of

engineering. The buildings, constructed from a combination of Martian materials and Anunnaki alloys, were designed to withstand the harsh conditions of the planet while providing comfort and safety to the inhabitants. Energy was abundant, thanks to the integration of Anunnaki zero-point energy generators, which powered everything from the colony's life support systems to its communication networks. The colony's central hub, a towering structure that housed the main command center and living quarters, was a beacon of light against the stark Martian landscape, its presence visible for miles around.

As New Horizons grew, so did its influence. The colony became a beacon of hope for humanity's future in space, attracting not just the brightest minds from Earth but also inspiring generations to dream of life beyond their home planet. Young people on Earth looked to the stars with renewed excitement, driven by the knowledge that they, too, could one day contribute to humanity's presence in the cosmos. The success of New Horizons sparked a wave of interest in space exploration, leading to the formation of new space agencies, private ventures, and international collaborations aimed at pushing the boundaries of what was possible.

The exploration of the solar system continued with fervor, driven by the technologies and inspiration provided by the Anunnaki. New spacecraft, equipped with advanced propulsion systems and navigational AI, embarked on missions to explore the outer planets, their moons, and even the asteroid belt. These missions, once fraught with danger and uncertainty, were now conducted with a level of precision and confidence that had been unattainable before the Anunnaki's visit.

On Europa, one of Jupiter's icy moons, a team of explorers established a research station to study the possibility of life beneath the moon's frozen surface. On Titan, Saturn's largest moon, another team began the construction of a permanent outpost, designed to withstand the moon's dense atmosphere and frigid temperatures. These outposts, though far from Earth, were connected to New Horizons and to each other by a sophisticated network of communication satellites, ensuring that humanity's reach extended across the solar system.

The solar system was no longer a distant dream; it had become humanity's new frontier. The colonies and outposts scattered across the planets and moons were just the beginning. Plans were already underway for missions to the outer edges of the solar system and beyond, as humanity, armed with the knowledge and technologies left behind by the Anunnaki, set its sights on the stars.

The journey that had begun with tentative steps on the Moon and Mars was now accelerating, driven by a collective sense of purpose and destiny. Humanity was no longer confined to its home planet; it was a species on the move, eager to explore, to learn, and to grow. The legacy of the Anunnaki had opened the door to the cosmos, and humanity, with its unquenchable thirst for discovery, was ready to walk through it, prepared to take its place among the stars. The journey continued, and with each new step, the future seemed brighter, filled with endless possibilities and the promise of new horizons yet to be explored.

Elon Musk, ever the visionary, had always believed that the future of humanity lay among the stars. His conviction was not merely a personal ambition but a deeply rooted belief that the survival and flourishing of the human race depended on its ability to transcend the boundaries of Earth. The visit from the Anunnaki had only strengthened this belief, providing the technological foundation and the inspiration needed to turn his dreams into reality. Armed with the advanced technology left behind by the Anunnaki, Musk set out to create something truly groundbreaking, an instrument that would forever change humanity's understanding of the universe.

This was not just any telescope; it was an instrument of unparalleled power, capable of peering deeper into the cosmos than humanity had ever conceived. The new telescope, aptly named *The Eye of Humanity*, was constructed in orbit around Mars, a location chosen for its optimal vantage point far from the interference of Earth's atmosphere and the light pollution that had hindered previous observations. The positioning around Mars, free from the gravitational constraints and atmospheric disturbances of Earth, allowed the telescope to achieve clarity and precision that was simply unattainable from any ground-based observatory.

The Eye of Humanity was a marvel of engineering, a testament to the fusion of human ambition and Anunnaki wisdom. Its massive, multi-segmented mirror, constructed from a lightweight yet incredibly durable Anunnaki alloy, was capable of reflecting even the faintest glimmers of light from distant stars and galaxies. The mirror's surface was a complex array of hexagonal segments, each one precisely calibrated to detect and focus light across a broad spectrum. This design, borrowed from Anunnaki principles of optical science, allowed the telescope to capture images and data with unprecedented detail and accuracy.

The telescope's sensors were equally advanced, utilizing a combination of human and Anunnaki innovations to detect not just visible light and electromagnetic waves but also subtle fluctuations in energy fields that could indicate the presence of advanced civilizations. These sensors were designed to scan across multiple dimensions, picking up traces of technology, energy signatures, and communication signals that would have otherwise gone unnoticed. The sensors could even detect the faint echoes of artificial constructs, remnants of civilizations that might have existed millions of years ago.

With this powerful tool, Musk and his team focused their attention on a specific and ambitious goal: the search for exoplanets that could harbor life. But their mission went beyond merely identifying planets within the habitable zone of distant stars. They were searching for signs of intelligent life, technological footprints that would reveal the existence of other civilizations in the cosmos. This included detecting energy signatures consistent with industrial activity, communication signals that hinted at advanced communication networks, and even artificial light sources emanating from cities on distant worlds.

The Eye of Humanity could detect the faintest traces of civilization, giving humanity its first real chance to answer the age-old question: are we alone in the universe? The data gathered by the telescope was vast, and it was transmitted back to Earth and Mars, where teams of scientists, engineers, and data analysts eagerly awaited each new batch of information. Sophisticated AI systems, many of them based on Anunnaki algorithms, processed the data, filtering out noise and identifying patterns that might indicate the presence of life.

The results were nothing short of astonishing. The telescope quickly identified hundreds of exoplanets with the potential to support life, many of which exhibited anomalies that hinted at the presence of advanced technologies. Some planets showed clear signs of atmospheric manipulation, others emitted energy patterns that could only be the result of artificial sources, and a few even displayed faint but detectable signs of communication signals, as if their inhabitants were reaching out across the void.

The implications were profound: humanity was not alone, and there were other civilizations out there, waiting to be discovered. The discovery of these planets reignited humanity's sense of wonder and adventure. The dream of finding other intelligent beings, of learning from them and perhaps even joining them in a larger cosmic community, was no longer a distant fantasy. It was a real possibility, within humanity's reach.

The lessons learned from the Anunnaki, lessons of cooperation, respect for all life, and the pursuit of knowledge, guided this new phase of exploration. Humanity approached this next chapter with a sense of humility and responsibility, aware that their actions would shape not just their own future but the future of countless other beings in the universe. *The Eye of Humanity* had opened a window to the cosmos, and through it, humanity could see the future: a future where the descendants of Earth would venture forth to explore the stars, forever changed by their encounter with the beings from Nibiru.

This telescope was not just a tool for exploration; it was a symbol of humanity's evolution, a declaration of their readiness to step onto the galactic stage. The journey that had begun on Earth, nurtured by the knowledge and technologies of the Anunnaki, was now expanding beyond the solar system. The discoveries made by *The Eye of Humanity* would shape the course of history, guiding humanity toward its destiny among the stars.

With the discovery of potential life-bearing exoplanets, humanity's focus shifted dramatically from the immediate concerns of survival on Earth and Mars to the boundless opportunities awaiting them in the vast expanse of the universe. This shift represented a profound transformation in the collective mindset of humanity, a transition from introspection and preservation to exploration and expansion. The Anunnaki's visit had not only provided humanity with the technological tools needed to venture into space but had also sparked a deep-seated yearning to connect with the greater cosmos, to seek out new life and forge relationships that transcended the confines of a single planet or star system.

The dream of a unified, advanced civilization, one that transcended the boundaries of Earth, Mars, and beyond, now seemed within reach, no longer a mere ideal but a tangible goal. The knowledge and technologies imparted by the Anunnaki had given humanity the confidence and capability to take its first steps into the wider galaxy, and these steps were taken with a determination and sense of shared purpose that had never been seen. The unity that had begun to form on Earth and Mars was now extending to the stars, driven by a collective ambition to explore, understand, and contribute to the broader tapestry of life in the universe.

New spacecraft, marvels of engineering and innovation, were designed and constructed to reach the exoplanets identified as potential cradles of life. These vessels, equipped with the most advanced propulsion systems humanity had ever developed, were powered by the Anunnaki's quantum drive technology, an innovation that made faster-than-light travel a reality. This breakthrough not only shattered the limitations of time and distance but also opened the door to regions of space that had previously been considered unreachable within a human lifetime. These ships were more than just machines; they were embodiments of humanity's aspirations, crafted with precision and purpose, ready to embark on missions that would take them to the farthest reaches of the galaxy.

Each mission was meticulously planned, reflecting the gravity of the undertaking. Crews were assembled with care, consisting of the finest scientists, engineers, explorers, and diplomats' humanity had to offer. These individuals were not chosen solely for their technical expertise but also for their ability to represent the best of humanity, their curiosity, their capacity for empathy, and their commitment to peaceful exploration and collaboration. These missions were as much about establishing connections with other species as they were about discovering new worlds; they were about continuing the journey that had begun with the Anunnaki's visit to Earth and carrying it forward into the unknown.

As the first of these ships prepared to depart from the Martian shipyards, a wave of hope and excitement swept across both Earth and Mars. People gathered to witness the launch, their eyes filled with wonder as they watched the massive vessels ascend, leaving the red dust of Mars behind. These ships, carrying the legacy of two civilizations, were more than just explorers; they were symbols of the unity and progress that humanity had achieved, monuments to what was possible when knowledge and technology were shared for the common good.

The missions ahead were not just about finding new worlds; they were about establishing connections, learning from other species, and continuing the journey that had begun with the Anunnaki's visit to Earth. These voyages represented the culmination of a dream, a dream that humanity could become a true member of the interstellar community, contributing its unique perspectives and innovations to the cosmos while learning from the civilizations they encountered along the way.

The descendants of Earth, now true citizens of the cosmos, ventured forth into the unknown, guided by the lessons of the past and the promise of the future. The encounter with the Anunnaki had forever changed the course of human history, igniting a passion for discovery and a commitment to building a better, more enlightened civilization. As humanity spread out among the stars, they carried with them the ideals that the Anunnaki had helped to instill, ideals of cooperation, respect for all life, and the unending pursuit of knowledge.

The journey into the cosmos was just beginning, but it was a journey filled with promise. The stars, once distant and unreachable, were now within humanity's grasp, shining brightly as beacons of hope and possibility. And as the first ships ventured beyond the edges of the solar system, the dream of a unified, advanced civilization, a civilization that could take its place among the stars, was no longer a distant hope. It was a reality, unfolding before their eyes, as the journey continued into a future filled with endless possibilities. This was the dawn of a new era, one where humanity was no longer bound by the limits of their home world but was free to explore the infinite, guided by the wisdom of their ancient allies and the boundless curiosity that had always driven them forward.

The End

Printed in Great Britain
by Amazon

fffb53ad-0bfd-467f-bc76-85612ba6bca4R01